"Listen to this," Lila said. "............ You're entering an emotionally and physically turbulent phase. Planetary activity is heavy this month as the Sun and that trickster Mercury pass through the most sensitive area of your chart. . . .'"

"Mercury! Gemini is *ruled* by Mercury!" tall, blond Amy Sutton said in alarm.

"So what?" Jessica said, turning to her.

"Don't you remember what the horoscope hotline said?" Amy asked. "Mercury is in retrograde."

"Mercury is in retrograde? What does that mean—it's backpedaling?" Winston inquired.

Lila, who had suddenly become an expert on the subject, said pedantically, "When Mercury is in retrograde, unconscious forces surface, and everything goes wrong."

"It's like Murphy's Law," Amy added, relaying what she'd learned from the hotline. "Everything that can go wrong, will."

Lila looked at Jessica meaningfully. "Boy, are you in trouble. I hope you don't have any big plans!"

"Oh, come on, Lila," Jessica scoffed. "Don't tell me that the movement of the planets is going to affect my actions. Maybe *you're* at the mercy of the stars, but *I'm* always in control of my destiny."

OPERATION
LOVE MATCH

Written by
Kate William

Created by
FRANCINE PASCAL

BANTAM BOOKS
NEW YORK · TORONTO · LONDON · SYDNEY · AUCKLAND

To Molly Jessica W. Wenk

RL 6, age 12 and up

OPERATION LOVE MATCH

A Bantam Book / March 1994

Sweet Valley High® is a registered trademark of Francine Pascal
Conceived by Francine Pascal
Produced by Daniel Weiss Associates, Inc.
33 West 17th Street
New York, NY 10011
Cover art by Bruce Emmett

ISBN: 0-553-29860-7

Published simultaneously in the United States and Canada

Bantam Books are published by Bantam Books, a division of Bantam Doubleday Dell Publishing Group, Inc. Its trademark, consisting of the words "Bantam Books" and the portrayal of a rooster, is Registered in U.S. Patent and Trademark Office and in other countries. Marca Registrada. Bantam Books, 1540 Broadway, New York, New York 10036.

PRINTED IN THE UNITED STATES OF AMERICA

OPM   0 9 8 7 6 5 4 3 2 1

Chapter 1

"Dame Fortune really has it in for you this month, Jessica!" Lila Fowler said, smiling as she looked up from the horoscope section of *Sweet Sixteen* magazine.

Jessica Wakefield looked at her best friend in amusement. "Oh, yeah?" she asked. "What does Lady Luck have to say?"

Jessica and Lila were surrounded by their friends Amy Sutton, Maria Santelli, and Winston Egbert at Casey's Ice Cream Parlor on Monday afternoon. They had decided to stop in for some cool refreshments after school to get out of the unrelenting heat. The usually balmy southern California town of Sweet Valley had been bathed in a heat wave for two weeks.

All eyes turned expectantly to Lila, who took a long draw on her root-beer float. "Well," she said slowly, savoring the attention, "it looks like Gemini is headed for a roller-coaster ride in the romance department. . . ."

1

"Did I hear Gemini?" Winston Egbert, the class clown, laughed. "The lovely Wakefield sisters are *Geminis,* the sign of the *twins*?"

"What else?" said Jessica, tilting her fountain glass back to get the last drop of her milk shake. "And with the way my love life has been going recently, I'd welcome a roller-coaster ride!"

"Listen to this," Lila said. "'Heads up, Gemini. You're entering an emotionally and physically turbulent phase. Planetary activity is heavy this month as the Sun and that trickster Mercury pass through the most sensitive area of your chart. . . .'"

"Mercury! Gemini is *ruled* by Mercury!" tall, blond Amy Sutton said in alarm.

"So what?" Jessica said, turning to her.

"Don't you remember what the horoscope hotline said?" Amy asked. "Mercury is in retrograde."

"Mercury is in retrograde? What does that mean—it's backpedaling?" Winston inquired.

Lila, who had suddenly become an expert on the subject, said pedantically, "When Mercury is in retrograde, unconscious forces surface, and everything goes wrong."

"It's like Murphy's Law," Amy added, relaying what she'd learned from the hotline. "Everything that can go wrong, will."

Lila looked at Jessica meaningfully. "Boy, are you in trouble. I hope you don't have any big plans!"

"Oh, come on, Lila," Jessica scoffed. "Don't tell me that the movement of the planets is going to affect my actions. Maybe *you're* at the mercy of the stars, but *I'm* always in control of my destiny."

"Just giving you a friendly tip," Lila said.

2

"Well, with Mercury in retrograde, we should *all* be careful," cautioned Amy.

"Yeah, it's a good week to just lay low," Lila agreed. "In fact, I think I'll put off my fabulous masquerade ball for at least two weeks."

"Aw," Winston said, pulling a sad face. "Maria and I were all set to come as the sun and the moon." Even though pretty, brown-haired Maria Santelli and lanky, knobby-kneed Winston Egbert really were like the sun and the moon in the looks department, their shared fun-loving natures made them a perfect match.

"You could still come as the Big Dipper," Lila retorted.

"I don't think we should even bother with shopping this afternoon," added Amy, famous for her avid mall-going tendencies. "Who knows? We could end up buying something really hideous!"

"What!" Winston exclaimed in mock horror. "No shopping? Maria, call the paramedics. Something's happened to Amy!"

"Hey, look who just arrived," said Lila, ignoring Winston and indicating the far corner of the ice-cream parlor. Jessica's heart flip-flopped. Michael Hampton, the new senior, had just sat down. Everyone at school had been buzzing about him all day. His family had just moved from the East Coast into a stately home in the hill section of Sweet Valley, the most prestigious area of town. The word around school was that his father was a documentary film-maker who had moved to California to direct a Hollywood movie. Michael himself looked like a movie star, *and* he drove a red Mazda Miata, a com-

3

bination that both Lila and Jessica found irresistible.

"Who's that?" Maria asked.

"Where've *you* been?" said Jessica, resisting the urge to crane her neck to get a better view. "That's Michael Hampton."

"Would you just look at him?" Amy said dreamily. "Have you ever seen anyone so gorgeous?"

Jessica had to agree with Amy. Michael was wearing faded blue jeans and a pale yellow T-shirt that contrasted with his dark skin and highlighted the contours of his well-defined chest. "Never," Lila sighed, drinking Michael in with her eyes. "Sandy hair and sea-green eyes. Sweet Valley's answer to James Dean."

Jessica listened in annoyance as Lila and Amy gushed about Michael Hampton. They had been making fools of themselves all day, falling over each other for his attention.

Looking over at Michael sitting coolly at his table, his long legs stretched out in front of him, Jessica sensed that gushing wasn't the way to Michael Hampton's heart. Taking him in, with his tall iced tea held lightly in his hand and the newspaper opened in front of him, Jessica felt she understood him: Michael Hampton was the epitome of cool. And the moment she'd laid eyes on him at lunch, Jessica had decided that he was the one for her.

"What do you think his sign is?" Lila asked.

"He must be a Leo," Amy speculated. "With those looks and that noble, leonine bearing."

"Yes, definitely a Leo, just like me," said Lila, tossing her mane of long brown hair. "Proud, majestic, confident . . ."

"Jealous, catty, lazy, hot-tempered . . ." Jessica added mischievously, unable to resist.

"Mee-oow!" said Winston, drawing a laugh from everyone.

"I think he's a Pisces," said Amy. "Mysterious, sensitive, dreamy . . ."

"Sounds a little fishy to me," Winston put in.

Jessica shook her head. "Michael Hampton is a Sagittarius," she said categorically.

"How do you know?" Amy asked.

"Because Sagittarians have great sex appeal," Jessica explained. "And they're perfect for Geminis."

"So I guess he'd be perfect for your sister, Elizabeth," said Lila archly.

"I think you've got stiffer competition than Elizabeth to worry about," Jessica retorted.

Lila's brown eyes narrowed to slits. "We'll just see about that. But the way your horoscope's going, I don't think you stand a chance."

You wish, thought Jessica, giving her a steely look. She opened her mouth to respond, but was struck by a sudden realization. *Elizabeth!* she thought in alarm. She had forgotten all about their meeting scheduled for that afternoon at school. "Ohmigod!" she said, jumping up and grabbing the astrology book Lila had loaned her the night before. "I've gotta go. See you!" Jessica swung her leather book bag over her shoulder and flew out of the restaurant. *Elizabeth's going to kill me!*

"I wonder what Jessica's excuse will be this time," Bruce Patman said, a note of annoyance in his voice. He and Elizabeth Wakefield had been waiting for

Jessica—who was predictably late—on the far side of the Sweet Valley High football field. Their secret meeting was scheduled to begin a half-hour ago.

"Based on Jessica's latest obsession, it'll probably be something to do with planetary alignment," Elizabeth surmised, dangling her bronzed legs from the bleachers.

"Planetary alignment?" Bruce scoffed.

"Jessica and her friends spent the entire evening last night huddled around the phone, calling 1-900-ZODIACS, the horoscope hotline. They're convinced that those predictions are the key to a successful love life," Elizabeth explained.

"That figures. Your sister always was a little spacey," Bruce said.

"Watch it, Bruce," Elizabeth said, raising her eyebrows. "You're talking about my identical twin."

Elizabeth felt obliged to stand up for her sister, but all the same, Jessica could be so exasperating! Sometimes Elizabeth felt as though she was Jessica's older sister by four years, not four minutes. It was just like Jessica to get caught up in some fad of the moment.

Elizabeth sighed. Jessica's momentary manias usually ended in disaster. Like the time Jessica had gotten taken in by the Good Friends cult and had had to be rescued by her friends and family. Or when she had joined Bruce's secret club, Club X, just to prove a girl could be as daring and courageous as a boy. She had almost gotten herself killed in the process.

Jessica and Elizabeth were identical in appearance, but only in appearance. At sixteen, they were five feet six and slender, with long, sun-streaked blond hair, sparkling blue-green eyes the color of the nearby Pacific, and lovely heart-shaped faces. They even had the same tiny dimple in their left cheeks.

But that was where the similarities stopped. In character, Jessica and Elizabeth were totally different. Jessica pursued her social life with an energy that left her sister breathless. She was co-captain of the cheerleading squad and an active member of Sweet Valley High's hottest sorority, Pi Beta Alpha. And if she wasn't doing splits or planning social functions, Jessica could always be found at the center of a crowd, either shopping at the mall, tanning at the beach, or practicing the latest dance at the Beach Disco, Sweet Valley's popular teen hangout.

While Elizabeth liked to have fun just as much as her sister, she was driven by more serious goals. She was a model student with ambitions to be a professional writer someday. As a reporter for Sweet Valley High's newspaper, *The Oracle,* Elizabeth devoted much of her free time to researching and writing articles and working on her "Personal Profiles" column. Unlike Jessica, who liked to take center stage, Elizabeth preferred quieter pursuits. In her spare time, she could usually be found talking with her best friend, Enid Rollins, walking on the beach with her steady boyfriend, Todd Wilkins, or recording her private thoughts in her journal.

Elizabeth thought of Jessica's latest craze with foreboding. Astrology *seemed* an innocent enough pursuit. But with Jessica, nothing remained harmless for long.

"It's hard to see with the glare from the sun," she said. The sun was just starting to sink in the clear sky, and its rays reflected sharply off the aluminum bleachers. Elizabeth dug around in her canvas book bag for her sunglasses, but all she came up with was a pink floral ponytail holder.

"Yeah, seems like this heat wave will never end," Bruce grumbled, wiping beads of perspiration off his forehead. "Jessica's probably hanging out in your pool, while we're sitting here, baking in the sun."

"She better not be at home," responded Elizabeth, twisting her golden-blond hair back into a ponytail. She squinted into the sun, searching for signs of her sister.

Bruce leaned in to get a better view of the field and brushed against Elizabeth's bare shoulder. They both jumped apart as if burned. Bruce coughed self-consciously, and Elizabeth looked away. *I guess we're both still uncomfortable after everything that happened last week,* Elizabeth said to herself, remembering with a blush. She and Bruce had been sure that Elizabeth's mother and Bruce's father were having an affair, and the whole thing had been so disorienting that they had convinced themselves that they were in love as well.

As Elizabeth stared out into the high-school football field, the green expanse blurred into the grassy quad at the university, where she and Bruce had spent an idyllic afternoon the week before, uncovering the details of their parents' college engagement. Upon Elizabeth's discovery of an old trunk in the attic containing a wedding portrait of Hank Patman and Alice Wakefield, she and Bruce had both jumped to the conclusion that their parents had once been married. When Mrs. Wakefield and Mr. Patman had gone to Chicago together for a business trip, Bruce and Elizabeth couldn't help but suspect them of having an affair.

The discovery had been earth-shattering for Elizabeth: Not only had her mother been married before, but now she was having an affair! But Elizabeth realized that the revelation had been even more devastating for Bruce, whose parents' marriage was definitely on the rocks. It had seemed as though nobody understood what Bruce and Elizabeth were going through, nobody but themselves.

We got more than we bargained for, Elizabeth thought. *We discovered an old romance between our parents, and a new one between us. To think I believed I was in love with Bruce, of all people,* mused Elizabeth in wonder. *Rich, arrogant Bruce Patman!* The son of Henry Wilson Patman, a rich, successful industry mogul, Bruce Patman was considered to be the best-looking and wealthiest boy in Sweet Valley. And he knew it. Jessica and Bruce had actually dated a few times in the past, and now they had a love-hate relationship. But Elizabeth had never been able to stand him.

She cast a sidelong glance at Bruce, sure he could read her thoughts. Just last Saturday night, she had actually found herself locked in an embrace with him in the Wakefield kitchen—right in the middle of a pool party that she and Jessica were throwing. Elizabeth thought back to the moment, to the current of energy that had run between them as they'd kissed passionately. *No doubt about it,* thought Elizabeth, shaking her head, *there was an irresistible charge between us.*

9

Afterward Elizabeth had realized that she had confused physical attraction with emotional attachment. She could never care for Bruce the way she loved Todd. On some level, she had been unconsciously living out the past, trying to reenact her mother's ancient love story with Hank Patman.

Bruce stared dejectedly into space. He felt as if his world had been turned upside down. His parents were on the verge of a messy divorce and his girlfriend, Pamela Robertson, had broken up with him after she'd realized he had fallen for Elizabeth. He hadn't realized Pamela was the girl he really loved until it was too late. First his parents, then his girlfriend. Was everything in his life destined to fall apart? Bruce wondered in despair.

Elizabeth shifted uncomfortably on the hard bench. "Maybe this wasn't such a good idea after all," she wondered aloud.

"Yeah," Bruce agreed. "Maybe Jessica's just too much of a ditz to be counted on."

Too hot to bother defending her sister again, Elizabeth sighed, willing Jessica to appear. "I really wish she'd get here," she said, tapping her foot impatiently. "I told Todd I'd meet him after his basketball practice." After the way she had treated her boyfriend the previous week, Elizabeth didn't want to be late. Todd had been very understanding about the whole affair with Bruce, but Elizabeth didn't want to push things. It couldn't have been easy for him, walking into the kitchen to find his steady girlfriend locked in a heated kiss with someone else.

"Yeah," said Bruce gruffly. "I've got a date too." He didn't see why he should mention that his date was with his cousin, Roger Barrett Patman, to play tennis at the Patmans' court. But he was still nursing a wounded ego. After Elizabeth had reconciled with Todd, Bruce had felt like a fool. He had dismissed his feelings for Elizabeth as a temporary delusion, but he actually had been a little in love with her. Witnessing the tender reconciliation between Elizabeth and Todd had been one of the more humiliating experiences of his life.

Bruce shook his head angrily, forcing his thoughts back to the present. *Where is Jessica?* he thought, anxious to hear her plan to get his parents back together. When Mrs. Wakefield had finally told them the whole truth about her relationship with Mr. Patman, everyone had decided that the next line of business was to get the Patmans back together. Knowing that Jessica was an expert on affairs of the heart *and* matters of manipulation, they had all turned to her for a plan.

Skeptical, Bruce had instinctively rejected the idea. *Jessica may be a master of maneuvering,* he had thought, *but only when she has her own interests at heart.* He had figured Jessica would be too irresponsible and self-centered to come through with a plan to help him. His instincts had clearly been right.

Bruce scowled and stood up, disgusted with himself for having harbored any hopes. "I'm getting out of here," he said impatiently, grabbing his backpack off the bleacher and swinging it onto his back.

"Bruce, wait, I think I see her!" Elizabeth exclaimed, putting her hand up to her forehead to shield her eyes from the sun. She felt a sense of relief as she saw her sister running across the field.

11

Jessica was coming toward them at full speed. Elizabeth gasped as she saw her sister drop the book she was carrying and trip over it, falling flat on her face on the thick grass of the field.

"Jess!" exclaimed Elizabeth, running over to pick her up. Bruce sauntered along behind her, looking irritated. Elizabeth extended her hand to Jessica, and Bruce retrieved her book, Linda Goodman's *Love Signs*. Jessica stood up shakily, her knee skinned and her face smudged with dirt.

"Pretty graceful, Wakefield," said Bruce, handing Jessica the big red book with a skeptical look.

"It's Lila's," Jessica told him, quickly putting the book in her leather book bag.

"What's with you, Jessica?" Elizabeth demanded. Jessica looked a little befuddled. "Why are you so late?"

Jessica brushed herself off and tried to think of a good excuse. She hated it when Elizabeth got more-punctual-than-thou, and she had to come up with something better than stopping off at Casey's for a soda. "You'll never believe this," she began, thinking it was a stretch but worth a try, "but I'm late because Mercury is in retrograde, and it makes absolutely *everything* go wrong!"

Bruce flashed Elizabeth a knowing look. "Pretty lame, Jessica."

"Really, Jessica," Elizabeth agreed. "A for originality, D for plausibility. You'll have to do better than blaming the planets. We've been waiting—"

"No, really," Jessica cut in, "when Mercury's in retrograde, it exerts a pull on the earth that makes things malfunction."

12

"Well, it's definitely exerting a pull on your brain, then," said Elizabeth impatiently. "Now, come on. We've got only a few minutes to figure out how to get Bruce's parents back together."

"What are we waiting for?" Jessica said, stalking purposefully up the bleachers. She sat on the top one and became all business. "I've come up with a plan— a foolproof plan." Jessica looked around the deserted field and lowered her voice to a whisper. "Operation Love Match."

Bruce rolled his eyes, but Jessica ignored him, pausing for a moment to let her words sink in. "There is only one means to the end—and that is the beginning," she continued dramatically. "Where—"

"Jessica," Elizabeth interrupted impatiently, "I think you've seen too many detective movies."

"Yeah, Jessica. Drop the theatrics and get to the point," added Bruce.

"You two are absolutely no fun," Jessica said. "You can't rush great plans. Just hold your horses. OK, Bruce, what's going on with their marriage now?"

"Well, Jessica," said Bruce bitterly, "right now they're probably on the phone with their divorce lawyers. That's what's going on with my parents' marriage."

"Right, but why?" Jessica urged. "Your mother thinks your father is having an affair with our mother, right? We know he isn't. But something must have gone wrong in their marriage to make her think that."

Bruce thought about it for a moment. "Well, actually, my father has been totally absorbed in his work—and I think my mother has been feeling neglected."

13

"It sounds like he doesn't appreciate your mother," Elizabeth remarked.

"Yeah," Bruce said thoughtfully. "He's always putting down her volunteer work because it doesn't make any money."

"Aha!" said Jessica excitedly. "He takes her for granted. Now we're talking. But first things first. We need to convince your mom that your father isn't having an affair with anyone, much less our mom."

"Why don't we just tell her?" Elizabeth asked.

"That, big sister, is why I am the master schemer, and not you," said Jessica, reveling in her role as ringleader. "She won't believe us, that's why. She needs to hear it from the source."

"So why doesn't Mr. Patman tell her?" Elizabeth asked.

"Why doesn't Mr. Patman tell her?" Jessica echoed, feigning astonishment at her sister's much too simplistic view of human nature.

"Yes, Jessica, *why not?*" Elizabeth asked again in an exasperated tone.

"Male pride, that's why," said Jessica triumphantly. "He's hurt that his wife would ever doubt him. What we have to do is make Mrs. Patman *think* that he told her he's not having an affair. It's just a question of how."

Suddenly Jessica's eyes lit up. *This astrology stuff might really come in handy,* she thought. *It's certainly worth a try!*

"Oh, no," Elizabeth groaned. "I know that 'sudden flash of inspiration' look."

"I don't know what you're talking about," Jessica said innocently. She quickly turned her attention back to Bruce. "Bruce, what's your mother's sign?"

"How should I know?" he responded curtly.

"When's her birthday?" Jessica persisted.

"It's uh, April twelfth, I think," Bruce said reluctantly.

"April twelfth—hmm, she's an Aries," Jessica reflected, ticking off traits on her fingers. "Aries are independent, bossy, stubborn, emotional, impulsive, impatient. . . ."

"Jess—" Elizabeth warned her.

"You know," Bruce said, considering, "that does kind of sound like my mother."

"See?" Jessica looked at her sister victoriously. "And your father's birthday?"

"July twenty-second," said Bruce.

"A Cancer! Of course," Jessica said, remembering what the hotline had said about "the crab." "Cancers are strong, forceful, tough, determined—but also moody, oversensitive, romantic, secretive, and difficult to understand."

She flipped excitedly through Lila's book until she got to the "Aries *Woman*, Cancer *Man*" section. She skimmed the section rapidly. "'Both of them are intensely jealous,'" Jessica read aloud. "'Each of these two Sun Signs is as fond of money, fame, and recognition as the other.'"

Jessica continued to peruse the page. "Listen to this!" she said in excitement. "'Another trouble spot could be this man's tendency to keep secrets. . . . When the Crab refuses to tell her what's on his mind, she may imagine all sorts of far-out things, and torture herself into a fit of Mars hysteria.'"

"I don't know how Mars fits in, but my mother has definitely tortured herself into a fit of hysteria,"

Bruce agreed, and Jessica remembered hearing how Mrs. Patman had impetuously moved out of the Patman estate a week ago. *This stuff really works!* she said to herself.

"Let's see," she said, thinking out loud. "She's emotional and determined; he's forceful but romantic." Suddenly she snapped her fingers. "I've got it!"

"What?" Bruce and Elizabeth exclaimed in unison.

"We'll just have old Hank write Marie a letter. A love letter," said Jessica. "Penned by yours truly, of course."

"Are you sure this will work?" Bruce asked skeptically.

"I promise you," declared Jessica solemnly, "within one week's time, your parents will be planning their second honeymoon."

Chapter 2

Jessica bounded through the screen door in a red string bikini, refreshed from the swim she had taken after she and Elizabeth got home from their meeting with Bruce.

"Hi, Dad." She kissed him on the cheek and then plopped down at the kitchen table, toweling her hair with a fluffy beach towel. "Welcome back to *Sweat Valley!*" She poured herself a tall glass of lemonade and drank it down in one gulp.

Ned Wakefield, who had just returned from a week-long ABA conference, couldn't help laughing, and Mrs. Wakefield shook her head. Then, taking in her daughter's outfit, she said, "Jessica, I know you're hot, but you'll have to put on a little more than that for dinner."

"OK," Jessica said, jumping up and flouncing out of the room. "But don't start without me!"

"Elizabeth! Soup's on!" called Alice Wakefield. Her shoes clattered on the Spanish-tiled floor of the

Wakefield kitchen as she carried a large covered pot to the table. She looked crisp and fresh in a petal-green linen suit.

"I hope we're not really having soup in this weather," Mr. Wakefield said, kissing his wife's cheek as he made his way to the table.

"Vichyssoise—cold soup," said Mrs. Wakefield, smiling. "And pasta salad."

"Not only are you a brilliant and thoughtful gourmet cook," said Mr. Wakefield, scattering place mats around the butcher-block table, "but a beautiful one at that."

Alice Wakefield, who had just returned from *her* business trip with Hank Patman on Saturday, did look stunning. The pale green suit complemented her slim figure and brought out the sparkle in her blue eyes. It was easy to see where the twins had inherited their fresh, all-American good looks.

"Mmm, something smells good," said Elizabeth, walking into the kitchen, her blond hair still pulled back in a high ponytail to keep her hair off her neck. "Dad!" she exclaimed. "I didn't know you were back!"

Elizabeth wondered if their mother had had a chance to fill their father in on the events of the last week. From the smile he gave her as she pecked him on the cheek, she guessed she hadn't. Not yet, any-way. She grabbed a stack of ceramic bowls sitting on the counter and carried them to the table. *Maybe Mom will just let it pass,* she thought, knowing it was only wishful thinking.

Mrs. Wakefield followed Elizabeth to the table with a colorful dish of cold, tricolored fusilli and sat down. Mr. Wakefield reached over and began serving the pasta.

Jessica raced back into the room and fell into her seat breathlessly. "I'm so hungry I could eat the entire state of California," she said, ladling some soup into her bowl.

"Well, I *guess* that's better," said Mrs. Wakefield, eyeing her daughter's skimpy purple cotton minidress.

"Yes, nightclub attire is definitely more appropriate *à table* than beachwear," joked Mr. Wakefield.

"Hey, Mom, did you know that Virgo women have to be careful about the spending habits of Sagittarian men?" Jessica asked, changing the subject to impart the latest wisdom she had picked up from her astrology book. "You better watch out. Dad might go on a spending spree and spend all your hard-earned money."

"I think Virgo women have to watch Gemini girls' wild pool parties when their parents are out of town," Mrs. Wakefield said dryly, causing both girls to closely examine their pasta salad.

"What's this?" Mr. Wakefield inquired, raising his eyebrows.

"Uh, Elizabeth and I just wanted to have a few people over to the pool, you know, to get out of the heat. . . ."

"Let me guess. Before you knew what was happening, the entire junior class and some extras showed up, and how could you possibly deprive them of the chance to swim in our pool?"

"Yeah, something like that," said Jessica, swirling her soup spoon in her vichyssoise, then looking up at her father guiltily.

Elizabeth remained silent, dreading what else Mrs. Wakefield would reveal about the girls' unchaperoned week. Todd's parents had been out of town as well, so Todd and Elizabeth had decided to try living together. Naturally, Mrs. Wakefield had found out, and Elizabeth knew she hadn't heard the last of it.

"Your father and I haven't had a chance to discuss this yet, but you girls know the rules, so after dinner your father and I will decide on an appropriate punishment."

The twins exchanged despairing looks.

"And there's something else I wanted to talk with you about," Mrs. Wakefield said, looking at Elizabeth.

This is it, she thought, bracing herself.

"I've been thinking about what I said on Saturday about coming up with a plan to get Bruce's parents back together," Mrs. Wakefield continued. "And I just don't think it's the right thing to do. I mean, we all want to help Bruce's parents, but we don't have the right to interfere in their personal lives."

Elizabeth was so relieved that her mother hadn't mentioned her little experiment with Todd that it took her a moment to comprehend what she had said.

"But I've come up with the greatest plan ever!" Jessica said enthusiastically. "His parents will be back together in no time." Elizabeth kicked her twin underneath the table.

"Ouch!" Jessica yelped. Elizabeth's jaw tightened. For all Jessica's cunning, sometimes she could be so dense.

"Did you hurt yourself, Jess?" Mrs. Wakefield asked in concern.

"No, it's nothing. Just hit the table leg," Jessica

grumbled, sending Elizabeth a dirty look.

"Mom, I thought we all decided—" Elizabeth said calmly, remembering her promise to Bruce.

"I know," said Mrs. Wakefield. "But I think we all got a little carried away at the time."

"Your mother's right," agreed Mr. Wakefield. "As a family, we've never believed in meddling in other people's private affairs, and I don't think this is the time to start."

Elizabeth stared down at her plate. They had promised Bruce they would write the love letter, and he was counting on them. He already felt so discouraged. How could she let him down? *Maybe we could just do this one thing,* she thought. She looked up at her sister, who nodded and gave her a knowing look. Sometimes Elizabeth felt that Jessica could read her thoughts.

"I mean it, girls, no interfering in Bruce's parents' affairs," Mrs. Wakefield said sternly, noting the look that had passed between them.

"OK, Mom," the twins said in unison.

"Hmm," Jessica pondered after dinner, staring at the blank computer screen as she prepared to compose Mr. Patman's love letter. "Something strong but romantic."

"Daring but understated," Elizabeth suggested, feeling slightly guilty about disobeying her parents' orders.

"Passionate but pragmatic," added Jessica.

The two girls burst out laughing.

Jessica sat propped up against the wall in her bed, Elizabeth's new laptop computer perched precariously on her knees. Elizabeth lay comfortably on the floor amidst a pile of Jessica's clothing, staring up at the ceiling. Jessica's bedroom had been a study in purple and silver ever since she had redecorated from her previous all-brown phase. The chaos in Jessica's room provided a stark contrast to Elizabeth's impeccably neat bedroom, done in shades of soft cream and beige.

"'Ma chère Marie,'" Jessica began composing out loud. "'I—'"

"C'mon, Jess, she'll never believe it," Elizabeth cut her off.

"You're right." Jessica began again. "'Marie, mon petit chou, light of my life, fire of my eyes—'"

"Jessica!" Elizabeth hurled a purple throw pillow at her. "We haven't got all night. I've got a date with Todd in twenty-five minutes, and I want to be out of the house before Mom and Dad decide I can't go."

"Yeah, I don't envy you right now," Jessica said with just a touch of smugness. "I can't imagine what your punishment will be. What's the penalty for living in sin with your boyfriend? Being grounded for ten years? A convent, perhaps?"

"Well," said Elizabeth, "I was hardly sinning. I think being grounded for a week should be plenty. In a way, we were only trying to be responsible—seeing what a more grown-up relationship would be like before we actually do it."

Jessica rolled her eyes, and Elizabeth knew she was unconvinced. To tell the truth, she hadn't really convinced herself, either.

"You should follow my angelic example," Jessica said, smiling and fluttering her eyelashes. "Then you'd stay out of trouble. Just ask yourself before you do something: 'Would Mom approve?'" she preached virtuously. "'Would Dad be happy about my—' Arrggh!" she shrieked as Elizabeth hummed another pillow at her head.

"Jess, the day I take model-behavior lessons from you is the day I get my head examined. Now, come on. Let's get this done."

"OK, OK," said Jessica. "How's this: 'My dear, darling Marie—'?"

"No, no, no. More realistic." Elizabeth sighed and lay back on a crumpled teal cotton jumpsuit.

"'Sometimes silence can send the wrong message—'" Jessica continued hopefully.

"No, something more poetic," Elizabeth interjected. "Let's see—'Sometimes silence can speak louder than words.'"

"I've got it!" Jessica said excitedly. *My dear Marie,* she typed. *Sometimes silence can speak louder than words, and in this case, I think my silence on the subject of our marriage has sent you the wrong message.*

Jessica paused, considering. "Hmm, how about: 'But I haven't said anything because—because I am hurt that you would doubt me'?"

"Make it more concise," Elizabeth proposed. "How about, 'But my pride and my hurt have been in the way'?"

Jessica nodded. *But my pride and my hurt have been in the way,* she added, typing rapidly.

"Hey, my pink T-shirt!" Elizabeth exclaimed, holding up a wrinkled scoop-neck cotton T-shirt with tiny pearls embroidered around the neckline. "I've been looking for this for weeks!" She stared at Jessica accusingly.

"Do you mind?" Jessica said. "The artist is at work." She continued to compose out loud, biting on the end of a fingernail. "'My love, you are the only woman I am interested in.'"

"Elizabeth!" called Mrs. Wakefield, knocking lightly on the door of Elizabeth's bedroom.

"Oh no!" Elizabeth said, bolting upright. "What are we going to do?"

"Shh," Jessica hissed. "Don't worry. I'll take care of it. We're in my room, Mom!" she called out. Mrs. Wakefield crossed through the bathroom adjoining the twins' bedrooms and walked into Jessica's room.

"Hi, Mom," said Jessica, smiling sweetly as her mother opened the door. Elizabeth stared fixedly at a poster across the room, avoiding her mother's eyes.

"What are you working on?" asked Mrs. Wakefield.

"Liz is helping me with my history paper for Mr. Jaworski," explained Jessica smoothly. "She's letting me try out the new laptop." Elizabeth had saved up for a laptop computer and had given Jessica her old word processor.

"Oh, that's nice, Liz," said Mrs. Wakefield, smiling at Elizabeth. Elizabeth swallowed hard and tried to smile back, achieving what felt more like a crooked grimace. "But remember, you're only *helping* Jessica with her paper, you're not *writing* it for her."

"Humph," grumbled Jessica. "Did you want something, Mom?"

"Oh, right. I knew I came in here for a reason," said Mrs. Wakefield. "Elizabeth, Todd just called while I was on the phone."

"Thanks, Mom," Elizabeth squeaked, feeling more guilty than ever.

"Don't work too hard, girls," said Mrs. Wakefield lightly, shutting the door behind her.

Elizabeth sank back onto the floor, sighing with relief. "I don't know if I can take it, Jess," she said. "I hate going behind Mom's back like this."

"You should be used to it, after last week," Jessica said unsympathetically. "Anyway, you're the one who promised Bruce we would help. I generously only offered my services to get you out of the tight spot you found yourself in—Bruce's arms." Jessica cackled with laughter at Elizabeth's enraged look. "Oh, stop it. Don't put on the prim act with me, Liz. I'm your twin, remember? There are no secrets between us," she said firmly. "We both know Bruce can be the biggest jerk on the face of this earth, we both know he's a fabulous kisser, and we both know that right now he needs our help. So smooth your ruffled feathers and let's finish this before your date with Mr. White Bread." She quickly scanned the screen and read back the last line. "'My love, you are the only woman I am interested in.'"

"No," Elizabeth said, swallowing her outrage with difficulty. "The idea is right, but the tone—" She thought for a moment. "'My love—I have eyes for you and only for you.'"

"OK," Jessica said, deleting the last line and typing in the new one.

My love, I have eyes for you and only for you. It is my work, and not another woman, that has driven us apart. Forgive me, Marie. Please tell me that it is not too late, that I haven't sacrificed the most important

things in the world to me—the woman I love, and . . .
Jessica hesitated. "'The wonderful family we have made together'?"

"I guess. If you can call Bruce a wonderful family," Elizabeth said wryly, then felt a twinge of guilt. She and Bruce had gotten quite close in the last few weeks, and though they would never be romantic again, she hoped they were now good friends. But sometimes it was hard to forget how she had always thought of him. "Try to make the sentence parallel," she suggested. "How about 'the woman I love and the family I cherish'?"

"Good, good," Jessica crooned, adding the last line. Quickly she ran a spell-check on it, then hooked the laptop up to the printer the girls shared. After showing the neatly printed letter to Elizabeth, who nodded her approval, she signed the letter with a flourish.

"Now for the finishing touch," Jessica said, her eyes gleaming. She dashed out of the room and returned a moment later with a bottle of her father's English Leather cologne. She folded the letter in thirds and inserted it carefully into an ivory envelope, sealing it with a gold sticker and dabbing it with a bit of her father's cologne for extra effect.

Leaving Elizabeth upstairs getting ready for her date with Todd, Jessica hurried down the steps to mail the letter. At the bottom of the stairs she collided with her father.

"Jess?" Mr. Wakefield said inquiringly. "Going somewhere?"

"Hi, Dad! Just doing a little stargazing. Be back in a sec," she said brightly, skipping out the front door.

It was a bright, clear night, and the sky was dotted with twinkling stars.

Jessica ran down to the corner mailbox, feeling triumphant and satisfied. It was a good thing that she and Elizabeth were doing for the Patmans. If her parents' marriage was in trouble, she would want someone like herself lending a caring hand—and a devious mind. She remembered her parents' brief separation a while ago. She had been devastated, and she, Elizabeth, and their older brother, Steven, had joined forces to get her folks back together.

We're old hands at this, she thought cheerfully, dropping the letter into the mailbox. She turned to head back to the house, but then stopped dead in her tracks. *The stamp!* she thought in alarm, clapping her hand to her mouth. *Liz will never let me live this down. What a typical Jessica move*, she thought in disgust. After all their hard work, and the cologne and everything.

Well, she wasn't going to give up that easily. Glancing around to see if anyone was looking, Jessica stuck her arm as far into the mailbox as she could to try to fish out the letter. But as hard as she tried, she couldn't even reach the masses of mail, much less the critical letter.

Giving up, she started to pull her arm out, but found she couldn't. Her bracelets had gotten caught on the shelf that dumps the letters. She was stuck! The harder she pulled, the worse it got.

I'm totally caught! she thought in dismay, looking around wildly for help. To her horror all she saw was a police car slowly cruising down the street.

Jessica gulped in panic. Keeping her eyes glued

on the approaching vehicle, she tried desperately to dislodge her hand. *This can't be happening to me. I just have to act casual. Maybe they won't notice I have my arm down the box,* she thought frantically. Just then she noticed a red Mazda Miata turn the corner.

Michael Hampton! she thought in dismay. *Is there any way this situation can get worse? How about an earthquake right now?*

Jessica tried to strike a casual pose, resting her left elbow lightly on top of the mailbox and leaning against it with her ankles crossed in front of her. Whistling and looking around nonchalantly, she tried to appear as if she were waiting for someone.

Just as Michael drove by, the police officer got on his loudspeaker and boomed, "Remove your hand from the mailbox! Remove your hand from the mailbox!"

Please, please, let the earth just open and swallow me up. Let me just disappear from the face of the earth forever. I cannot believe this. Jessica was so embarrassed she wanted to die. *Just my luck,* she thought. *The man of my dreams drives by, and like an idiot I have my hand caught in a mailbox, and now I have Officer Friday bellowing at me. This is just fabulous.* She desperately tried to extricate herself, but to no avail.

The police officer pulled over and got out of his car. Jessica thought she saw Michael Hampton watching the spectacle through his rearview mirror. *How will I ever live this down? I won't, that's how. I won't, ever.*

"Do you realize that tampering with the mail is a

28

federal offense, young lady?" the police officer asked sternly.

"Uh, yes," Jessica answered in a rush, desperate to get rid of the police Officer as quickly as possible. "But you see, officer, I—I wasn't actually *tampering*. It's just that I mailed an *extremely* important letter and I forgot the stamp, so I just *had* to get it back, and then my hand got caught—"

"The details are irrelevant," the police officer interrupted her firmly. "An offense is an offense."

"Of course, Officer," she said, quickly changing tactics. She flashed him a winning smile. "You are completely right," she said in her most complacent tone, "and I'll never—"

"I'm taking you down to the station, young lady," interrupted the officer again. "Now, get in the car."

Jessica's composure snapped. "I would love to, Officer, but my *hand* is *stuck*. I've been *telling* you. If you'd like to get my hand unstuck, I'll be happy to go with you to the station. Or maybe we could just take the mailbox with us," she said sarcastically, aware that she was sinking into hotter water all the time. *Dad is going to love this. Hope he's not too tired from his trip.*

Jessica and the officer were locked into a battle of wills as they stood there, glaring at each other. Then, with a sick feeling in the pit of her stomach, she noticed Michael begin to back up the street toward them.

Michael stopped his car and got out. Jessica forgot all about the policeman for a minute and gazed at Michael. He looked cool and together in soft, faded jeans and a white cotton shirt. Then, remembering her predicament, she froze, mortified that he was seeing her in this ridiculous situation. She could feel

29

her face burning as he calmly shut the door to his car and strode unhurriedly toward them.

"Is there a problem here?" Michael asked softly, smiling down at Jessica.

Jessica shook her head. "Uh, no, no problem—"

"Seems the young woman's gotten herself stuck," offered the police officer, apparently believing her story. Jessica looked away, flushed with embarrassment, wishing she could disappear into one of the cracks in the sidewalk.

"Hmm," said Michael, coolly assessing the situation. He joined Jessica at the mailbox, standing so close to her that she could feel the heat from his body.

"It's my bracelets . . ." Jessica said weakly, aware of his clean, soapy scent.

Michael reached down into the mailbox and clasped his hand around Jessica's wrist, gently removing the offending jewelry. Jessica shivered, her hand tingling from his touch.

Well, that's it, she thought as she pulled out her arm. *My chances with him are finished.* Then she had an idea. Elizabeth would kill her if she found out, but she had no choice.

She turned to Michael with a shy smile. "Thank you for your help," Jessica said demurely. "I'm Elizabeth Wakefield, by the way." He just nodded his head, looking at her with his incredibly sexy green eyes. Then he handed her her bracelets and got back in his car.

"This way, Ms. Wakefield," said the police officer sharply, taking her arm and escorting her to the car. "We're going down to the station for fingerprinting."

Chapter 3

"Todd, Todd, wait!" said Elizabeth, gasping with laughter as she tried to pull back from his fervent embrace. "My hair—my hair's caught in the seat belt!"

Elizabeth had managed to run out of the house without her parents' saying anything, and she and Todd had driven up to Miller's Point, a romantic parking spot overlooking Sweet Valley. Before he'd even put the car in park, Todd had wrapped Elizabeth in his arms and engulfed her in a passionate kiss.

Reaching over, he undid the clasp to Elizabeth's seat belt and carefully untangled her hair from it. Then he covered her throat in tender kisses, traveling slowly up her neck to her ear. He dropped featherlight kisses on her cheeks and her eyelids, sending shivers up Elizabeth's spine.

Elizabeth closed her eyes and turned toward him, returning his kisses with the same ardor, happy just to lose herself in the moment, to let her thoughts about her impending punishment and Bruce's parents fade away in the hot night air.

"Hair OK?" Todd asked with a smile as they pulled back for air. He reached over and smoothed down the golden-blond locks flowing loosely around Elizabeth's shoulders.

"All better," said Elizabeth, smiling back.

"Wow, it's beautiful up here. We're really all alone," Todd said, looking around the grassy hilltop. There wasn't a car in sight.

"The view is perfect tonight," Elizabeth agreed, gazing out at Sweet Valley bathed in moonlight below them. The charming southern California town glittered like a jewel.

"And so are you," said Todd in a husky voice, folding her in his arms and kissing her again.

"Oh, Todd." Elizabeth pulled back slightly with a sigh. "It seems like it's been so long since we've been together like this."

"Yeah," Todd teased. "We better not decide to live together again, or we'd *never* see each other."

"I'm afraid you're right," Elizabeth said ruefully, thinking back to the previous week.

At first the idea of Todd moving into the Wakefield house while their parents were out of town had seemed perfect. They would be together twenty-four hours a day—just like a married couple. Except at night, of course, when Todd would sleep downstairs on the couch. So with Todd's parents away on vacation, and both Mr. and Mrs. Wakefield gone on business, it had seemed the perfect opportunity for Elizabeth and Todd to spend all their time together.

But I ended up spending more time with Bruce

than Todd, Elizabeth remembered. The events of the previous week flooded into her mind, filling her head with a maze of confused images: Bruce's arms wrapped around her in the harsh light of her kitchen, Bruce's mouth passionately exploring hers, Todd's face as he stood in the doorway, Todd's car screeching off into the night. Then her reckless dive off the diving board, and the shock of hard, cold water, then blackness, utter blackness . . . and finally Todd's face looking down at her, Todd's arms holding her, warmth . . . peace . . . reassurance.

Elizabeth shook her head, longing to get rid of the memories forever. *Why did things have to get so complicated?* she thought. She wasn't exactly *sorry* she had kissed Bruce Patman—at the time, they had really seemed to need each other. But she did wish that she had never caused Todd such pain.

Elizabeth looked over at Todd, overwhelmed with love and appreciation for him. His strong, handsome profile was highlighted in the moonlight. He had been so understanding about the whole thing, thought Elizabeth in retrospect. Thank heavens he had accepted her explanation. Now they were closer than ever.

"It's so good to be with you, Todd," said Elizabeth, snuggling up to him. "Away from all the problems with Bruce."

"What problems with Bruce?" Todd asked suspiciously, pulling back and sitting upright.

"You know, the problems with his parents," Elizabeth elaborated. "His mother moving out, meetings with divorce lawyers . . ."

"Liz, I don't see what that has to do with you," Todd protested.

33

"Todd," Elizabeth said placatingly, "you were there when we all decided to come up with a plan to get Bruce's parents back together."

"We decided to have *Jessica* come up with a plan to get Bruce's parents back together," Todd corrected.

Elizabeth's cheeks flushed. "Todd, I explained about me and Bruce. You're not still angry about it, are you? Bruce is a friend, and I've always tried to help my friends. You have to trust me."

Todd's jaw tightened and he stared out the window.

Elizabeth bit her lip and looked out her own window.

"Liz, you're right, you—" Todd began.

"Todd, I'm sorry, I—" Elizabeth said at the same time. She took a deep breath and turned to face him. "I know we've been through a rough patch lately. But you have to believe me." The blue eyes she turned to him were beseeching. "I love *you*. The romantic feelings I had for Bruce were an illusion. I know that you're the boy for me." She smiled, looking into his wary brown eyes. "But please try to understand. I promised Bruce that I'd help him."

He reached across the car seat and took her hand in his. "Never mind, Liz. You don't have to explain. I trust you." He stroked her hair off of her face. "I know you love me, and I love you, too. As long as we're together, nothing else matters."

"Yeah, I know," said Elizabeth softly. "And Bruce really needs our help now."

"*Our* help!" Todd yelped.

"Yes, our help," said Elizabeth firmly. "I want you

34

to support me in this. I *need* you to support me in this," she amended. "It's important to me, Todd."

"Well," Todd said, "I do kind of feel sorry for Bruce. And I guess I can't blame him for wanting to be with you last week. I mean, who wouldn't want to be with the most beautiful girl in Sweet Valley?" Todd pulled her close to him and covered her lips with his. "And the most interesting girl in Sweet Valley," he continued, whispering between kisses. "And the smartest, and the sexiest, and the most altruistic, and . . ."

"And the luckiest!" said Elizabeth, her eyes sparkling. She leaned toward him to kiss him again.

Much later that evening, Elizabeth walked exuberantly in the front door of her house, her face glowing. It felt so good to have things back to normal again with Todd. She paused for a moment in the foyer, puzzled by the house's silence.

"Hello! Anybody home?" she called.

"Elizabeth, we're in here," her father called from the living room.

Uh-oh, Elizabeth thought, her mother's words at dinner suddenly coming back to her. *This is it!* Elizabeth walked into the living room to find her parents sitting together on the sofa and Jessica slumped dejectedly in an armchair, an embarrassed look on her face. Mrs. Wakefield was sitting up straight with her legs crossed, and her father was wearing a light windbreaker, as though he'd been out.

Nope, Elizabeth thought with foreboding as she took a seat in a chair near her sister. *This doesn't look good.*

"Dad, why do you have your jacket on?" she asked.

"Oh, I just got back from fetching Jessica from the police station," her father said lightly. Jessica squirmed in her seat, her face flushing.

"What?" Elizabeth gasped, looking from her father to her mother.

"Your sister was trying to retrieve a letter from the mailbox," explained Mrs. Wakefield. As her mother recounted the evening's events, Elizabeth's heart started thumping in her chest. Were they in trouble for trying to help Bruce?

"They wanted to press charges," said Mr. Wakefield, taking over from his wife, "but my law firm has done so much work with the precinct that they just let Jessica go with a warning." Mr. Wakefield looked at his daughter sympathetically. "I think they were just trying to scare you, Jess," he said.

"But that's not why we're here," said Mrs. Wakefield. Elizabeth's heart began pounding so loudly that the sound of it filled her ears. Had Jessica told her parents what the letter was? She held her breath as she waited for an explanation.

"We're not concerned with Jessica's letter. After all, Cara Walker is in London," Mrs. Wakefield continued. "Of course Jessica is going to write to her." Elizabeth let her breath out in a rush. "We're concerned with last week's, er, escapades."

"We're both grounded," Jessica burst out. "For a whole week."

Ned Wakefield spoke in a calm voice. "For holding a pool party here on Saturday night without our knowledge or our permission."

"That means no dates, no visits to the mall, no

parties," said Alice Wakefield firmly. "But of course, Jessica is free to go to cheerleading practice, and you can stay after school to work at *The Oracle,*" she added, her voice softening.

"But it's not fair!" Jessica protested. "How come Elizabeth and I get the same punishment when she was the one who had her boyfriend living with her for a whole week?"

"Jessica, that's enough," said Mrs. Wakefield, throwing her a stern look. "I believe you were the one tampering with the federal mail tonight."

Jessica sank down into her chair, looking as if she had been dealt a fate worse than death.

"As for you, Elizabeth," said Mrs. Wakefield, turning to her briskly, "we've discussed the fact that you decided to practice living with your boyfriend at the age of sixteen."

Elizabeth swallowed hard and her face turned red. But she sat up straight in her chair and held her head high, ready to accept her punishment with dignity.

"We've decided that you will do all of the chores this week, including making dinner, doing the laundry, taking out the trash, and cleaning the house," said Mrs. Wakefield.

Elizabeth grimaced, but nodded. "That sounds fair," she said, relieved to lessen the burden of guilt she felt at having deceived her parents the week before.

Jessica's eyes lit up when she heard Elizabeth's punishment. For once her perfect sister was in more trouble than she was. *And I won't have to do any chores for a week,* she thought gleefully. Then her face fell as she remembered her own punishment. She wouldn't have anything at all to do, since she couldn't go out, she realized glumly.

Jessica stood up suddenly. "Can I go to my room now?" she asked.

"Of course, dear," said Mrs. Wakefield.

"Good night, honey," added Mr. Wakefield.

Jessica pecked her parents on their cheeks in an obligatory manner and made her way slowly out of the room, looking like a wilted flower.

"'Night Mom, 'night Dad." Elizabeth jumped up after her and raced up the steps, impatient to get all the details of the love-letter fiasco.

"OK, Jess, let's have it," said Elizabeth, following Jessica into her room.

Jessica sighed melodramatically and flung herself on the bed. "This has been the worst night of my entire life," she declared. Elizabeth smiled in spite of herself. For Jessica, there was rarely any middle ground. No matter what event occurred in her life, it constituted either the best or the worst of all possible worlds.

Elizabeth shoved a pile of clothes aside and sat down on the desk chair. "So what happened? I want all the gory details."

Jessica quickly filled Elizabeth in on the evening's events.

"I can't believe Michael Hampton drove by just as you were standing there with your hand in the mailbox," Elizabeth said, chuckling.

"I know," said Jessica. "I've never been so humiliated in my whole life!"

"Well, at least you got to meet him," Elizabeth pointed out optimistically.

38

"Uh, right," Jessica mumbled, having neglected to tell Elizabeth that she had claimed to be her.

"Well, we're just going to have to call an emergency meeting to come up with Plan Two. How about tomorrow at lunch?" Elizabeth suggested.

"Plan Two!" exclaimed Jessica.

"Jessica, you told Bruce you'd help him come up with a plan," Elizabeth reminded her.

"Exactly," said Jessica. "A plan. Well, I came up with a plan and it didn't work. So now I've done my duty." Jessica had a determined look on her face. There was no way she was going to waste her time helping Bruce Patman. Especially now that Michael Hampton was in the picture. Jessica had more important things to worry about—like the way Lila was dying to dig her claws into him. "Besides," she added, thinking quickly, "Mercury is in retrograde. If we tried to help Bruce this week, it could end in total disaster. I mean, just look what happened tonight. First my hand got stuck in the mailbox, then I was taken down to the police station like a common criminal, and now we're grounded. And this is only the beginning."

"Oh, no you don't," Elizabeth said, refusing to take the bait. "You're not going to weasel your way out of your agreement with Bruce."

"I am *not* trying to get out of it," Jessica responded indignantly. "I'm just saying that the timing is bad. Maybe next week—"

Elizabeth looked at her sister, considering. "You know what I think?" she said finally.

"What?" asked Jessica.

"I think you're scared," Elizabeth declared.

"Me? Scared? Ha."

"Yep, scared. You're afraid you won't be able to get Bruce's parents back together. Your reputation as master manipulator is at stake," Elizabeth said.

"I am not scared!" said Jessica hotly. "I could easily get Bruce's parents back together."

"Oh, of course you could. We all know that. But if you didn't . . . Well, I guess it doesn't matter if Bruce thinks you've lost your touch." Elizabeth paused for a moment to let her words sink in. "You know, I think I saw him talking to Michael Hampton today at school. But I'm sure he would never mention to Michael that your spark is gone." She shook her head, pretending to mull over the situation. "No, I'm sure he wouldn't. And you wouldn't care anyway, right?"

"There's no way Michael Hampton would be friends with Bruce Patman!" Jessica said.

"Why not?" Elizabeth asked. "After all, they're both seniors. They're both rich. They both live on the hill."

Jessica hesitated, considering the situation. If Elizabeth was right about Michael and Bruce becoming friends, then it was definitely in her best interest to stay on Bruce's good side. Jessica rubbed her hands together. *Hmm,* she thought, *Bruce's parents' reconciliation could turn out to be the key to Michael Hampton's heart. If Bruce is going around singing my praises . . .*

"So," she said, "what time did you say we were meeting tomorrow?"

Chapter 4

". . . and then a police officer accused her of tampering with the mail and took her down to the station," Elizabeth said in a low voice to Bruce, updating him on the previous evening's events during lunch on Tuesday.

"He took her in?" Bruce said in a disbelieving tone.

Bruce and Elizabeth were sitting in the cafeteria, waiting for Jessica with her usual lunchtime crowd. This meant they had to suffer through Lila's and Amy's newfound belief in astrology. Caroline Pearce, the class gossip, was sitting across the table from them, chattering away merrily with Jeannie West and her best friend, Sandra Bacon.

Elizabeth looked at Caroline anxiously and drew her head closer to Bruce's. Bruce didn't want anybody to know what they were up to, and if Caroline got hold of the news, it was sure to travel through the school like lightning.

41

"Yeah," Elizabeth continued, lowering her voice. "My father had to go down to the station to talk the policeman out of pressing charges."

"How could she mess up something as simple as mailing a letter?" Bruce asked, exasperated.

"Planetary alignment, I suppose," Elizabeth responded humorously. She didn't tell Bruce that Jessica actually *had* blamed the evening's events on Mercury.

"Geez, you'd think—" Bruce began.

Lila's voice cut through their conversation. "Hey, you guys look pretty cozy over there," she said insinuatingly. Elizabeth was well aware that Lila knew all about the kiss between Bruce and Elizabeth at the pool party Saturday night, as did most of the junior class. It was the juiciest morsel of information to hit the gossip channels in a long time, Elizabeth thought ruefully. She could just hear Lila and Caroline hashing it through: "Not only are Bruce and Elizabeth the most unlikely pair at Sweet Valley High," she imagined them saying, "but conventional, conservative Elizabeth Wakefield acted entirely out of character."

Thinking about it made the blood rush to Elizabeth's face. She took a deep breath and looked straight at Lila. "Did you have something to say to us, Lila?" she asked in a controlled voice.

"No, no, just making a little remark," said Lila innocently.

"Well, maybe you should keep your little remarks to yourself," Bruce said, his voice harsh.

"My, we're defensive today, aren't we?" said Lila huffily.

Annoyed with the conversation, Bruce turned

away and surveyed the tables around him, looking for Pamela. Pamela had been sitting with Lila and Amy, but she had pointedly left the table when Bruce and Elizabeth had arrived. He saw her sitting a few tables away, talking quietly with some members of the girls' tennis team. After she had transferred from Big Mesa High, Pamela had become the new star of the Sweet Valley High team. Bruce tried to catch her eye, but she steadfastly avoided his gaze.

"Where the heck is your sister?" Bruce growled, turning his attention back to the table and looking at his watch.

"I can't imagine what's keeping her," Elizabeth said.

"She's probably caught in some Mercurial predicament," Lila speculated. "There's a total lunar eclipse in her sign today."

Bruce looked at Elizabeth and rolled his eyes.

"That goes for you too, Liz," Lila put in, giving Elizabeth a significant look. "I'd lay low today if I were you."

"Thanks for the tip, Lila. I'll be sure to lay very low," Elizabeth said wryly.

"No problem," Lila said with a wave of her hand.

"Oh, Lila," Amy said, her slate-gray eyes flashing with excitement. "I found out Jason Wynter's sign. He's a Capricorn."

Jason Wynter was the new tennis pro at the Sweet Valley Country Club. He was a senior at Bridgewater High School and drove a shiny red BMW. Lila and Amy had been checking him out at the country club lately. He had green eyes, thick blond hair, and an incredibly sexy smile.

"How did you find out?" Jeannie asked excitedly.

"I just went up to him at the club yesterday, and I said, 'Hey, what's your sign?'" Amy said.

"Brilliant," Bruce muttered.

"A Capricorn!" Lila breathed. "Capricorns are perfect for Leos. That's it—I'm asking him out."

"You're asking a guy out?" asked Winston, who had just arrived with Ken Matthews. "Ladies and gentlemen, a liberated woman of the nineties," he said, setting down his tray.

"That horoscope number, 1-900-ZODIACS, said my keys to success this month were action and aggressiveness," Lila asserted.

"You've been calling 1-900-ZODIACS?" Ken asked. "You're spending *money* on this astrology bunk now?"

"For your information," Lila said huffily, "astrology is a science. Besides, it's only a dollar per call."

"Yeah," Amy joined in. "And it's amazingly accurate. It said my cerebral activity would be at its peak this week, and I got an A on my math test."

"That *is* amazing," Bruce whispered to Elizabeth.

"And it said Sandy was in for a week of passion and romance," said Jeannie, "and Scott showed up five minutes later with a dozen long-stemmed roses."

"When Jeannie called in, it warned that Virgos would be accident-prone this month," added Sandra. "The very next day she sprained her wrist in cheer-leading practice."

Jeannie held up her bandaged wrist as proof.

"It's a miracle!" exclaimed Winston.

"Wonders never cease," Ken agreed.

Lila shook her head self-righteously. "You boys

are just too immature to understand."

"Much too immature," agreed Amy.

"Us? Immature?" Ken asked, crossing his legs and assuming an exaggeratedly sophisticated position. Winston adopted a blasé expression and pretended to blow smoke in Ken's face. Lila and Amy couldn't help laughing.

"Definitely," said Lila disdainfully. "I think we girls need some older, more mature, *senior* guys."

"Senior guys? Winston, she's wounding me," said Ken, pretending to thrust a sword in his chest.

"Hey, Lila, take it easy, would you?" said Winston. "He's sensitive, you know?"

"Oh, Win, I'm sorry," said Lila with exaggerated concern. "You know, just one more year and you're there. But for the moment . . ." Lila's practiced eyes raked the cafeteria.

"Yes, we absolutely need some senior guys," Amy said, picking up the clue from Lila. "Some suave, sophisticated seniors."

"Like tall, fair, and handsome Michael Hampton, for example?" asked Ken. "Ooh, he's sooo dreammy!" he said, fluttering his eyelashes.

"A real dreamboat," added Winston for good measure.

"Yes. Like Michael, for example," said Lila matter-of-factly. She looked over her shoulder at Michael, sitting alone, as usual, at a table in the corner. "You don't see *him* acting like an infant."

"I bet he's incredibly refined," breathed Amy. "He'd probably take you to La Maison Blanche on your first date and order everything in French."

Elizabeth looked over at Michael while the girls

scrutinized him. She was startled to find him staring straight at her with an intense expression on his face. Elizabeth shook herself and drew her attention back to the group. *He can't be looking at me,* she thought. *He doesn't even know me.* Yet every time she looked up he seemed to be casting glances in her direction.

"Hey, didn't expect to find you here at Jessica's table," Todd said, setting his tray next to hers and bending down to give her a quick kiss.

"Todd!" Elizabeth said, her face lighting up. "I thought you'd be busy with basketball practice."

"No, we're just meeting after school—afternoons and evenings," Todd explained. He was taking part in a week-long midseason basketball camp. Todd was the star of the Sweet Valley High Gladiators and was accustomed to putting in long, arduous hours of practice.

"Afternoons and evenings!" Elizabeth exclaimed. "Between your basketball camp and my being grounded, we'll never get to see each other."

"We'll just have to make the most of it when we do," said Todd, nuzzling Elizabeth's neck.

Bruce scowled.

"Oh, hi, Bruce," Todd said, noticing him for the first time.

"Wilkins," Bruce bit out. He pushed back his chair abruptly. "Look, I'm getting out of here," he said to Elizabeth. "Your flaky sister is clearly not going to show up."

"Wait," Elizabeth said, anxious to keep the peace. "We'll come with you to history class. Right, Todd?"

"Sure," he said agreeably, grabbing his burger off his tray and gathering his books.

Elizabeth, Todd, and Bruce left the cafeteria together and made their way through the crowded corridor toward their lockers. Elizabeth was pleased at how Todd was trying to be friendly to Bruce. She squeezed his hand as Bruce shuffled alongside them with his shoulders hunched and his head down, mumbling complaints about Jessica's irresponsibility. "I knew this was a bad idea," he grumbled. "Can't count on her for anything."

"I'm sure Jessica has a good reason for not showing up," Elizabeth said, sounding more confident than she felt.

Suddenly they heard a muffled voice. "Help!" "Help!" the voice said. "Get me out of here!"

Elizabeth looked around, alarmed. "Do you hear that?" she asked the others.

Bang! Bang! Bang!

"It's coming from Jessica's locker!" exclaimed Elizabeth.

"Somebody's in there!" Todd said.

"Help, please help! Somebody help!" came the voice again, louder.

"It's Jessica!" Elizabeth said, recognizing her sister's voice.

"Geez, Wakefield's locked herself in," Bruce said.

They hurried to Jessica's locker. "Jessica, we're coming!" Elizabeth called.

"How could she get stuck in her locker?" marveled Todd, shaking his head in wonder. "It's just not possible. It's literally impossible to do."

Bam! Bam! Bam! The locker door shook. Jessica's books and belongings were scattered all over the floor.

"Cut the racket, would you," Bruce snapped. "We get the picture."

"It's jammed shut," Elizabeth muttered as she tried in vain to pull up the metal handle of the locker door.

Todd wedged his English notebook into the crack of the jammed locker door, trying to pry it open slowly. Suddenly the door sprang open and a red-faced Jessica came flying out, landing on the pile of books and papers on the floor.

"Ohmigod, I almost got asphyxiated!" she exclaimed, dramatically gulping for air.

"Jessica, what happened?" Elizabeth asked, concerned but at the same time finding it difficult not to laugh at the spectacle her sister was making. "Did somebody lock you in?"

"Lock me in?" Jessica said, looking at her sister as though she were crazy.

"Then how did you get in there?" Elizabeth asked, incredulous. "And why are your books all over the floor?"

"I was looking for my English composition," Jessica explained, beginning to calm down. "I knew it was in there, and I just had to find it. Mr. Collins will kill me if it's another day late. But I couldn't find it in any of my books."

"So you decided to empty your locker and hide, in case Mr. Collins happened by," Bruce hypothesized. Mr. Collins, though Sweet Valley High's most popular English instructor, was notoriously exacting when it came to getting work in on time, so it wasn't such an outlandish idea.

"I wasn't *hiding*, Bruce," Jessica said evenly. "I was *trapped*."

48

"So what happened, Jess?" Elizabeth urged.

"I finally found my paper, but it was stuck in a corner of my locker, you know, in one of the cracks at the top. I had to sort of wedge myself in there to get it. Then a huge crowd of football players walked through the hall and knocked the door shut by mistake. . . ." Jessica explained.

"Hey, Liz, this could make the front page of *The Oracle*," said Bruce with a grin. "'Jessica Wakefield Found in Locker. Football Team Arrested.'"

"It's not funny, Bruce. I could have suffocated in there!" Jessica said indignantly.

"Well, did you at least retrieve your English composition?" asked Todd.

"Yep. See?" Jessica said proudly, holding up a mangled piece of paper with a tear across the middle. Just then she spotted Michael Hampton standing with a small group of seniors across the hall, watching them. *He must have seen everything,* she thought in despair. Her heart started thumping loudly in her chest, and bright pink circles popped out on her cheeks. "Oh, Jessica," she said loudly to Elizabeth, "I'm so glad you came!"

Elizabeth stared at her in amazement. "Are you sure you're all right? Maybe the lack of oxygen has really gotten to you."

"I'm fine," Jessica hissed. "Keep your voice down."

Elizabeth looked at her anxiously. "Look, Jess, we'll take care of your books," she said, indicating the contents of Jessica's locker scattered across the hall. "Why don't you just go ahead to class and sit down?"

"Thanks, Liz!" Jessica whispered, grateful to escapé from the awkward situation. She gave her sister a quick squeeze and ran off.

"Hey, Bruce," said Todd, as he and Elizabeth began to gather together Jessica's books, "do you think you could give us a hand?"

Bruce cast a disdainful glance at Todd and began picking up books. "Beautiful, this is just beautiful," he muttered to himself as he threw Jessica's books randomly into her locker. "Jessica doesn't show up for our meeting, Jessica locks herself in her locker, and now *I'm* cleaning up after her!"

Chapter 5

"This way, Bruce," Elizabeth said, guiding him through the crowd at the Dairi Burger Tuesday afternoon. She had just spotted Jessica sitting at a coveted corner booth. Since their lunch meeting had been a nonevent, they had decided to reconvene at the Dairi Burger.

"It's way too crowded here," Bruce said, looking around the restaurant in dismay. He had been hoping they would be able to talk alone. If they were seen by any of their friends, that would be impossible. *At least Wilkins isn't joining us,* he thought. *With any luck he'll be busy with his little basketball camp all week.* That way he'd be spared the humiliation of seeing him with Elizabeth. Not to mention how lonely their billing and cooing made him feel. Longingly he thought of Pamela, then quickly banished her from his mind. He'd blown it with her, and that was that.

The wooden booths and tables were jammed with

their schoolmates talking animatedly and devouring the Dairi Burger's famous burgers, fries, and milk shakes. A group of sophomores was huddled around the jukebox, arguing about what song to play next. Even the game room was packed, resounding with bleeps and pings from the video games and peals of laughter from the participants.

"I know, I think everybody from Sweet Valley High must be here," Elizabeth said, ducking her head as she noticed Enid sitting with her boyfriend, Hugh Grayson, at a small wooden table across the room.

"Oh, no!" said Bruce. "There's Roger and Ken! And Caroline with Amy and Barry."

"Just keep your head down and look straight ahead," Elizabeth advised as they edged their way surreptitiously through the throng of young people.

They made their way unnoticed through the crowd and slipped into the booth with Jessica, whose head was stuck in her *Love Signs* book.

"Oh, hi, Jessica, glad you could make it," Bruce said sarcastically. "I thought you might have gotten locked in your car."

"Very funny," Jessica said.

"Or zipped up into your cheerleading bag," Bruce went on.

Jessica didn't look amused. "Sometimes you can be so childish," she said.

"And sometimes you can be so klutzy," returned Bruce.

Jessica gave Bruce a dirty look, but refrained from commenting. She was wondering if she would have the perseverance to endure his obnoxious personality, but she had seen Michael Hampton at a corner table when she had walked in, and that had stiffened her resolve to impress Bruce with her cunning. "Now, listen to this. It's about a Cancer man," she said, reading aloud from Lila's book. "'Of course, it's equally true that his Crab-like trait of hanging on, when it comes to love, is an indication of his inclination toward loyalty and faithfulness.'"

"Jessica, don't you think we've got more important things to discuss?" Elizabeth asked, relieved to see her sister back to normal.

"More important?" protested Jessica. "What could be more important? This is the *proof* that Bruce's father isn't having an affair."

"Well, somehow I don't think it will convince my mother. And time is pressing, Jessica," said Bruce, a note of urgency in his voice. "My parents are meeting with their lawyers, the Traceys, in the morning, and—"

Bruce stopped talking as the waitress appeared. They placed their orders quickly. Bruce ordered a double cheeseburger and onion rings. Elizabeth just ordered an iced tea. Ever since this heat wave had begun, she hadn't had much of an appetite. The waitress set down a plate of fries and a strawberry shake in front of Jessica.

"Sorry, I went ahead and ordered without you," Jessica said apologetically, indicating her food. "I was kind of hungry."

Bruce nodded his head impatiently. "So, as I was saying," he continued as soon as the waitress was out of earshot, "my parents are meeting with their lawyers tomorrow. They've already separated—

53

Mom's been living in a house across town for a week. Now they just have to make it legal and it's all over."

"Well, we just can't let that meeting take place, can we?" said Jessica confidently.

"But how in the world can we stop it?" asked Elizabeth.

"Simple," Jessica said. She waved a fry dramatically in the air, knocking over her strawberry shake. The thick pink liquid flowed smoothly across the table and made its way toward the edge of the table. Jessica jumped up quickly and bumped Bruce's water glass with her elbow. The ice water spilled out of the glass just as the strawberry shake dripped all over Bruce's tan cotton pants.

"Nice work, Einstein," said Bruce, standing up and wiping himself off.

Jessica glowered at him, grabbing all of the paper napkins out of the metal holder on the table and frantically mopping up the mess.

Elizabeth ran to find the waitress, who arrived promptly with a busboy in tow. Jessica sat stony-faced as they efficiently wiped up the table and mopped the floor. "Did you have to call an army?" she hissed to her sister.

"We're so sorry," Elizabeth told the waitress graciously. "Thanks so much for your help."

"No problem," she said, smiling. "Accidents happen."

"Yeah, Jessica," Bruce said when the waitress had gone. "You're an accident happening."

"Well, at least I'm happening," Jessica retorted. "And not a dull, stuffy bore like *some* people I know."

"OK, OK," said Elizabeth, holding up her hands.

"We didn't come here to bicker. We came here for a reason."

"Humph," said Jessica, getting fed up. Here she was wasting her time with Bruce when she could be dazzling Michael in the corner. "Well, *I* certainly didn't come here to be insulted. Especially when I'm doing someone a favor." She glared at Bruce, who glared back.

"C'mon," said Elizabeth patiently. "Jessica, Bruce, let's call a truce."

"A Bruce truce," Jessica said, laughing at her rhyme.

Bruce wasn't amused. "Could we just get on with it?" he said in an irritated tone.

"Yeah," agreed Elizabeth. "So what's the plan?"

"Well," said Jessica, "let's get the facts straight first." She paused for a moment, considering the situation. "OK," she said to Bruce, "so your parents are meeting with their lawyers, the—what's their name—the Terrys?"

"The Traceys," Bruce said, rolling his eyes. "Martin and Jan Tracey. I can't believe you haven't heard of them. They're a very well-known husband-and-wife lawyer team with a sterling reputation. They're very good friends of my par—" Bruce stopped. "Or, they were . . ."

"Who's representing whom?" asked Elizabeth.

"I think Mr. Tracey is representing my mom, and Mrs. Tracey is representing my dad," Bruce said.

"That's interesting," Elizabeth said. "They're sticking up for the opposite sex."

"So your parents are meeting with Jan and Marty tomorrow morning," Jessica said, impatient to get on with their meeting. "Do you know what time their appointment is?"

"I think it's scheduled for ten o'clock," said Bruce.

"At the lawyers' offices?" asked Elizabeth.

"Yeah, at the Traceys' office downtown," confirmed Bruce.

"Hmm," said Jessica, considering the situation. "Tomorrow morning your parents are going to be together for the first time all week. So what we want to do is make sure that meeting takes place—"

"But I thought you said—" Bruce interrupted.

Jessica held up a hand. "Patience, patience. What we want to do is make sure that meeting takes place *without* the Traceys. Now, do you know how they're getting to the meeting?"

"Yeah, I think they're going to fly," Bruce said sarcastically, flapping his hands like wings. "They're going to *drive*, Jessica," he continued. "In their *cars*."

"OK, so we get rid of the Traceys. And *then* . . ." Jessica paused, her mind clicking with ideas.

"Jessica, I hope you're not planning to take the Traceys hostage or something," Elizabeth joked.

"Oh, Liz, really. That would be much too obvious. Now, Bruce," Jessica said, turning her attention to him, "is there anything in your house that would be meaningful to both of your parents?"

"You mean, besides money?" he asked sardonically.

"No, you moron, I mean like memories—old letters, books, special gifts, wedding pictures . . . That's it!" Jessica said suddenly, her eyes on fire.

"Jessica, tell us!" Elizabeth said, unable to contain herself any longer.

Jessica looked around stealthily and drew them in, lowering her voice to a dramatic stage whisper. "Here's what we'll do . . ." she said. They huddled together at the table, plotting out the details of Jessica's plan.

"Plan Two goes into action tomorrow," Jessica barked out sharply as the meeting adjourned. "Phase one, five A.M., phase two, nine A.M."

"And remember," added Elizabeth, "this doesn't get past the three of us." She gave Jessica a significant look.

"Why are you looking at me?" asked Jessica innocently.

"We'll make a pact," said Bruce. "The secret handshake." He crossed one arm over the other, extending his left hand to Elizabeth and his right hand to Jessica. Jessica and Elizabeth followed his example, crossing their arms over each other. The three of them all linked hands and solemnly lifted their arms into the air. A couple at a neighboring table looked at them strangely.

"Shall we synchronize our watches?" Elizabeth asked, her eyes twinkling.

"And you think *I've* watched too many detective movies?" Jessica asked.

"Jessica, you said it yourself, precision is everything," Elizabeth protested.

"All right, all right," Jessica agreed.

"It's five twenty sharp," said Bruce as they all set their watches by the old wooden clock on the Dairi Burger wall.

"Anyone need a ride?" Bruce offered, standing up to go. "I have to get back to school for tennis practice."

"No, I've got to get home," Elizabeth said. "Jessica and I are sort of grounded for the week. I told my parents I was staying at *The Oracle* after school to work on my 'Personal Profiles' column. But I guess I'll have to write it at home, because they won't believe it if I stay out much later."

"Jessica?" Bruce asked.

"Uh, no thanks," Jessica said, smiling sweetly. "I think I'll just stay here and do some reading. I'm sure I can catch a ride home with someone." *Like Michael,* she thought. "Oh, and Liz," she added. "Would you tell Mom and Dad I had to stay late for cheerleading practice?"

"Sure, no problem," Elizabeth said, sighing. "I'm sort of getting used to lying and sneaking around." She stood up and dug her keys out of her purse. Although the twins shared the Jeep, they each had their own set of keys.

Jessica eyed Michael sitting in his corner booth. He was sitting alone, drinking coffee and reading a large bound manuscript. With his aloof expression and sophisticated air, he looked as if he belonged in a café in Paris. *This is my chance!*

"Suit yourself." Bruce shrugged, walking away. "Later, Liz." Jessica noticed that he nodded hello to Michael as he left.

"See you at home, Jess," said Elizabeth.

Jessica waved good-bye, and Bruce and Elizabeth threaded their way out of the crowded restaurant. As they neared the front door of the restaurant, Bruce recognized a familiar mane of glossy, blue-black hair, and his heart flip-flopped. Pamela was sitting at a booth with Amy Sutton. "Pamela," he said softly, approaching her table with Elizabeth. She turned quickly at the sound of his voice. *She looks more beautiful than ever,* Bruce thought, gazing at her midnight-blue eyes, luminous in her pale face. Bruce felt elated as Pamela's eyes lit up for a moment. But as soon as she noticed Elizabeth, he saw them cloud over with hurt.

"Oh, hi, Bruce," she said coolly, and quickly turned back to her friend.

"Hi," he returned shortly. "C'mon, Liz, let's go." He brusquely turned away from the table and cursed himself for ever thinking that she might take him back.

As soon as Bruce and Elizabeth were safely out of sight, Jessica picked up her books and waltzed confidently over to Michael's table, rehearsing her opening lines on the way. *"Hey, you must be Michael, I'm Jessica."* No, too trite. *"Michael Hampton, right? Jessica Wakefield, nice to meet you."* No, too forward. *"Hi, Michael, Jessica Wakefield."* Perfect.

"Hi, Michael," she said, casually slipping into the bench opposite him. "Jessica Wakefield." She extended her hand graciously.

"Michael Hampton," he returned shortly, shaking her hand.

"I just wanted to welcome you to Sweet Valley. It must be so—*tiresome*—to adjust to a new environment," said Jessica in a debonair tone.

"It's all right," Michael replied.

"I also wanted to thank you for freeing my sister from her—uh—*unfortunate* circumstance yesterday," said Jessica, flipping her blond hair off her shoulders. "She's just so *awkward,* always getting into trouble." She laughed lightly.

Michael blushed slightly.

Hmm, he's obviously interested, Jessica thought. "And that incident at school this afternoon. The poor dear, locking herself in her own locker. I mean, really," Jessica said with just a hint of an English accent.

"You're not from around here?" Michael asked, a quizzical look on his face.

"Well, actually, I am," Jessica admitted. "But you know," she said in a confiding tone, leaning in close to him, "sometimes I feel so misplaced. I mean, Sweet Valley can be so, you know, *provincial.*"

"I suppose," Michael said, shrugging.

That didn't go over big. Well, just keep the conversation moving. "I thought you'd agree. So, what brought you to California?" she asked, eyeing the manuscript curiously.

"My father is a filmmaker," Michael explained. "He got an opportunity to make a Hollywood film. So here we are." He shrugged his shoulders.

"What's the film about?" Jessica asked, her interest piqued.

"It's a psychological thriller," said Michael.

"And you're reading the screenplay?" she asked.

"Uh, yeah," said Michael, quickly closing the manuscript.

Jessica wanted to press Michael further for details about his father's movie, wondering if he needed any actresses, but she bit her tongue. She didn't want to seem too obvious. "I suppose you're from New York?" she asked.

"Boston, actually," said Michael.

"The East Coast. I knew it," Jessica said. "I've always wanted to move to New York. But Liz, well, she prefers a small town. Oh, waiter!" Jessica said, flagging down a passing waiter. "A double espresso, please.

"But you know," she prattled on, "that's how it is with twins. We're Geminis, of course, but complete opposites. Seems likes Liz is always getting caught in jams and I'm always getting her out of them. She's rather clumsy and gauche, and I'm, well . . ." Jessica looked away modestly, allowing her voice to trail off.

Michael took a sip of his coffee.

"So, what are you into?" Jessica asked brightly. "Sports, I suppose."

"Uh, no, I'm not into sports," Michael said.

"No? I'm on the cheerleading squad myself, co-captain, actually. Poor Liz isn't on the team," Jessica said, neglecting to mention that Elizabeth hadn't tried out. "But you know, it really takes a lot of coordination and stamina."

"I'm sure," said Michael, looking at his watch.

Jessica panicked, searching frantically for something to say as an awkward silence filled the air. Fortunately the waiter arrived with Jessica's espresso. Jessica waited patiently as he placed her coffee on the table in front of her, giving him a condescending smile.

"I suppose you're going to join Phi Ep," Jessica said once the waiter was gone.

"Phi Ep?" said Michael.

"Phi Epsilon," Jessica explained. "It's the coolest fraternity at Sweet Valley High."

"Oh, right. Bruce Patman told me about it."

"Oh yes, Bruce. He's absolutely one of my best friends. He's the greatest. Anyway, I'm a member of

Pi Beta Alpha, Sweet Valley's most exclusive sorority. I used to be president, but you know, it's just so *hard* to fit everything into one day."

Jessica paused to take a sip of her espresso, almost choking from the bitter taste. "But enough about *me*," she said. "We were talking about *you*. You were telling me what you liked to do."

"Uh, me? Not much of anything, actually," Michael said.

"Now, you must do something," Jessica said, pouring three sugars and two creamers into her espresso. "I have a slight sweet tooth," she explained hastily.

"Well, I like to write, actually," Michael said, amused by her attempts to sweeten the coffee.

"You—write?" Jessica said, aghast, thinking of her sister's avid interest in journalism. "Like newspaper articles?"

"Oh no, nothing journalistic. Just fiction—you know, short stories and plays and stuff," Michael explained.

"Oh, of course," Jessica said, quickly regaining her composure. "I'm into the theater myself. Not that I wouldn't like to get into film. In fact, I just played the lead in Sweet Valley's production of *Macbeth*. David Goodman directed it—you must have heard of him," she said, barely pausing for breath.

"No, I don't think I have," said Michael.

"Well, anyway, the play got rave reviews. I'm planning to make my debut on Broadway as soon as I get out of school," Jessica said. "Or to land a role in a film," she added quickly.

"Great, great," Michael said, nodding.

Finally, thought Jessica, *a common interest.* "But

I've still got another year of school before I can start my career," Jessica continued. "Another long year." She sighed dramatically and looked away.

"Uh, if you'll excuse me," Michael said, standing up abruptly, "I've got to get going. It was nice talking to you." He swung his book bag over his arm and headed for the door.

Jessica stared after him, completely baffled. *Did I come on too strong? Was I too enthusiastic? Maybe I should play it even cooler,* she thought, downing her espresso.

Michael steered his Miata through the winding streets of the quiet town, deep in thought about Sweet Valley High. Sororities, fraternities, cheerleading, sports. It seemed as though all the kids played a sport here. And it seemed as though everybody had a huge group of friends. Michael had never been very interested in sports. He had never been good in groups, either. He sighed. He would never fit in here.

His school in Boston had been so different—much more staid and conservative than Sweet Valley High. He had been more in his element there. Michael had been the editor of the yearbook. One of the plays he had written had been performed the year before. But even then, Michael admitted to himself, he'd felt awkward and out of place.

Michael drew a deep breath. He'd always been a bit of a loner, spending much of his time by himself, thinking and writing. The other guys in his class had seemed so comfortable together, always ribbing each other and throwing playful punches. They had been comfortable with girls as well. Michael had always envied their confidence and security.

When Michael found out that his father had been given the opportunity to direct a Hollywood movie, he had made a serious resolution. In California, he had told himself, he was going to be a different person. Nobody knew him there. Nobody knew that he was shy and insecure and that he thought about things too much. In Sweet Valley, he could make a new start. He would be cool, confident, outgoing.

But now he wasn't so sure. California really was the land of sun and surf—full of tanned, muscular guys like Bruce Patman and pretty blond girls like blue-eyed Jessica Wakefield. Popular, bubbly Jessica Wakefield practically oozed California confidence. Her sister Elizabeth seemed more his type. He thought of how embarrassed she'd been to have her hand stuck in the mailbox. Then today she had managed to get herself trapped in her locker. And that was no easy feat! Michael laughed out loud, thinking of it. Maybe he should ask her out. No, he would probably make a fool of himself, stammering awkwardly as he always did. She would just laugh in his face and walk away. Michael sighed. He had always been too shy to ask anyone out. The only times he dated girls was when they took the initiative.

Well, that's all going to change now, Michael said to himself. He drove through the Sweet Valley hills, strengthening his resolve. Boston was for the old Michael. From now on, he would be a new man.

Chapter 6

"Jessica," Elizabeth hissed in Jessica's ear. "Get up! It's time."

"Five A.M.," Jessica grumbled, squinting at her alarm clock. "Whose idea was this, anyway?" She sat up slowly and hit the button on her alarm clock automatically, knocking the clock off the bedside table. The clock fell to the floor with a loud clatter. Jessica groaned and dropped back into bed, burrowing under the covers.

"C'mon, Jess," Elizabeth urged, retrieving the alarm clock and setting it on the nightstand. "Bruce will be here any minute."

"I don't think I slept at all last night," Jessica said, making another effort to sit up. She had been completely wired after her meeting with Michael. The double espresso hadn't helped.

"Do you want me to make you a cup of coffee?" Elizabeth offered.

"I don't even want to think about coffee," Jessica

said, stretching her arms above her head and rubbing her eyes.

"She's up! She's sitting!" Elizabeth teased.

"So bright and cheery at this hour," Jessica muttered, sliding her legs onto the floor and standing up. She made her way groggily to the bathroom to wash up. In the bathroom, Jessica stared at herself in the mirror. Her normally glowing smooth face was pale and puffy, and her hair was standing on end. She groaned and picked up her toothbrush.

"Here, wear this," Elizabeth said when she emerged, handing her a pile of clean clothes.

"I can't believe I'm up at five o'clock in the morning for Bruce Patman. I must be getting soft in my old age," Jessica griped as she pulled on a pair of jeans and a heavy gray sweatshirt and slipped her feet into a pair of white tennis shoes. She grabbed her keys from her dresser and shoved them in her pocket.

Elizabeth handed her a hairbrush.

"Bruce owes me big-time," Jessica grumbled on, running the brush hastily through her hair.

"C'mon, Jess, let's go," Elizabeth said, taking her arm and leading her out the door. They made their way carefully downstairs, speaking in hushed voices.

"How did I ever let myself get talked into this?" Jessica complained as they crept down the stairs.

"Jess!" Elizabeth whispered. "Keep your voice down!"

They inched cautiously across the living-room carpet and pulled back the curtains to check for Bruce.

"No Bruce," said Elizabeth, peeking out the window. "Hey, it looks like it's going to rain. Maybe this means the heat wave's finally breaking."

"Nothing like lovely sunny southern California at five in the morning," said Jessica, looking out at the overcast day. The sky was dark and stormy, threatening with big black rain clouds, and the sun was hardly in evidence at all.

"Yeah," Elizabeth said. "Perfect weather for espionage."

"We're going to get soaked." Jessica sighed, plopping herself down on the bottom step of the staircase.

Elizabeth rummaged hastily in the coat closet and grabbed one of Mrs. Wakefield's scarves and a battered old overcoat that her father had worn in college. "Here," she said, holding them out. "Take your pick."

Jessica stared in horror at the choices and reached out warily for the pink scarf. It was made of a translucent gauze material and had "Alice" written all over it. "You've got to be kidding," Jessica said, holding it up. "How could Mom own something so tacky?"

"Jessica, nobody is going to see us! It's five A.M.," Elizabeth said.

"Well, it's just the principle of the thing," Jessica said, but her protest was cut short by the sound of a low horn.

"It's Bruce!" Elizabeth exclaimed. "C'mon!"

Jessica and Elizabeth carefully shut the front door behind them and ran out into the early-morning drizzle as Bruce pulled up in his black Porsche. He opened the passenger door quietly and the girls climbed in.

"Hi, Brucie, baby!" Jessica said brightly, remembering her vow to stay on his good side. She settled back comfortably in the passenger seat as they got on their way.

"Wow, what a personality transformation," said Elizabeth.

"Hi, Jessica, sweetie," Bruce said sardonically. "Hey, Liz," he added, twisting around to greet her.

"Hi, Bruce," Elizabeth said, giving him a warm smile. "I guess this is it!"

"Yeah, Bruce. Your parents are going to get so gooey looking at their wedding pictures that they'll probably leave for their second honeymoon before you get home from school."

"Hrmph." Bruce maneuvered his Porsche over the deserted Sweet Valley streets. "Here," he said, indicating a couple of glass bottles of Coke sitting on the front seat. "I brought Cokes."

"Cokes?" Jessica asked in amazement. "At five in the morning?"

"I thought you might need some caffeine, Jess," Bruce said acidly. "Since you obviously didn't get your beauty sleep." Anxious about the upcoming day, Bruce was in a particularly foul humor, and in no mood for Jessica. His parents would be furious if they knew what he was up to. His father was spending a lot of money on the lawyers' fees for this meeting and was taking the morning off from work to attend it. He certainly wouldn't appreciate having his precious time and well-earned money sabotaged by Bruce and his two amateur partners in crime.

Jessica shrugged, twisting the cap off one of the bottles. "Did you steal these out of your father's Coke machine?" Jessica asked, taking a swig.

"Wakefield, do you always need to be such a pain?" Bruce said, wondering for the twentieth time how he had ever gotten himself into this situation.

"Hey, Bruce, did you get the Traceys' address?" Elizabeth asked, trying to change the subject.

"Yeah, I found it in my father's briefcase last night," Bruce said. "I did a trial run after dinner. Should be around twenty minutes."

Bruce turned onto Valley Crest Drive and sped smoothly through the Sweet Valley hills. He turned on the windshield wipers as rain began to pour down in a steady stream.

The wipers seemed to beat in time to his thoughts about his parents, drowning out the sound of Jessica talking next to him. Even if their plot did manage to keep the Traceys at bay, he thought, leaving his parents together in the same room could lead to utter disaster. His mother and father couldn't even live in the same house together. Why should being stuck in a cold lawyer's office be any better?

"Bruce, I asked you a question," Jessica said. "Didn't you hear me?"

"No," Bruce retorted. "Were you yammering about something?"

Jessica laughed. "Looks like someone's in a stormy mood."

Bruce glowered at her and put his foot on the gas.

Elizabeth's heart went out to Bruce. She knew what he must be going through. Not only was Bruce meddling in his parents' personal affairs, but in their business concerns as well. Poor guy, she thought. He could be getting himself into deep water.

"So, Bruce," Elizabeth said, trying to make conversation. "What do you think of the new senior—Michael Hampton?"

"Cool guy," said Bruce. "I think I might nominate him for membership in Phi Ep."

Jessica's ears perked up. So Bruce really *was* becoming friends with Michael. She shook her head in wonder. How could anyone be friends with Bruce? *Well,* she thought, *ours is not to wonder why!*

"So," she said briskly, instilled with a new sense of purpose, "let's do a quick checklist for today's plan. Elizabeth—Krazy Glue?"

"Check," said Elizabeth.

"Bruce—bird whistle?"

"Check," he said.

"Rubber gloves?"

"Check."

"Wedding album?"

"Check," said Bruce, a determined look in his eye. He gunned the engine and drove steadily on.

"That's it!" Bruce said a few minutes later, indicating a pink, Spanish-style estate with stucco walls and a wooden veranda in front. He cut the engine and coasted up to the driveway.

"The Traceys," Elizabeth affirmed, reading the name engraved in bold black letters on the mailbox.

"Aa-ttchoo!" Jessica sneezed loudly as they pulled up.

"Jessica, shh!" Elizabeth reprimanded her.

"Hrrmmph," Jessica griped. "I'm obviously catching a cold from running around in the rain at dawn, and you're complaining."

"Oh, that's likely," Elizabeth said, rolling her eyes. "You're catching a cold in this heat?"

70

"I told you what 1-900-ZODIACS said about this week for Geminis—bad luck in love and health. A good week to just crawl into bed and hibernate," she said firmly.

Elizabeth was beginning to lose patience. "Jess, I swear, if I hear *one* more word from you about the sun or the stars or planetary alignment, I'll, I'll—" Her voice trailed off as she searched for an appropriate threat.

"Fine by me," Jessica said, shrugging, "but don't say I didn't warn you."

"Here, Jessica," Bruce said, apparently trying to make amends for his grumpy behavior earlier, "take my raincoat."

"Well, at least *somebody* here has some compassion!" Jessica sniffled, throwing her sister a forlorn look. She unbuckled her seat belt and wriggled into the raincoat. "Hey, nice," she whistled, twisting around to read the label. "Burberry's of London."

"Only the best for poor little rich boy Bruce Patman," he said, cracking a crooked grin. "All ready?" He handed the girls matching pairs of yellow rubber gloves that he had found in the pantry. This way they couldn't leave any fingerprints.

"Ready," Jessica and Elizabeth answered together, pulling on the gloves.

"Be careful," Bruce said. "And remember, if you hear the signal, come back immediately." The warning signal was a shrill whistle that sounded like a birdcall. Jessica and Elizabeth got out of the car silently and crept toward the Traceys' twin Saabs. Bruce watched as Jessica and Elizabeth snuck furtively forward in the early-morning rain. *With Elizabeth in that old overcoat and Jessica in my raincoat,* he thought, *they look like private detectives out of a late-night movie.* Bruce stood guard in his Porsche, ready to give the signal should anyone appear. *I hope this works,* he thought nervously. The last thing he needed was to be arrested.

Elizabeth and Jessica stopped between the cars and looked at each other.

"I'll take the red one, you take the blue one," whispered Elizabeth, nervously handing Jessica a vial of Krazy Glue. Jessica nodded.

Elizabeth bent down to look at the cars. "They're unlocked!" she said in relief.

"Thank the stars for safe, secure southern California," Jessica said, grinning.

Elizabeth turned to the red car.

"Wait!" Jessica stopped her, hit by a sudden thought. "What if the alarms go off?" she asked.

"They're unlocked, Jess," Elizabeth explained. "The alarms aren't set."

What were they chatting about in the middle of the Traceys' driveway? Bruce thought in consternation. He breathed a sigh of relief as they headed to their respective cars.

Elizabeth crawled into the front seat of Mr. Tracey's red Saab and slid in behind the steering wheel. The dashboard seemed to stare at her, its modern knobs and controls glistening. Elizabeth's heart started beating loudly. She, Elizabeth Wakefield—proper, upstanding Elizabeth Wakefield—was about to commit a crime. She was going to vandalize somebody's property. Elizabeth hesitated and looked through the window at Jessica, who appeared busy at

72

work. *Well,* she thought, trying to reassure herself, *it is for a good cause. And the damage will be minor.* She knew neither was a justification, but she also knew she was going to do it anyway.

Elizabeth unscrewed the vial of Krazy Glue with shaking hands. Inching carefully around the steering wheel, she brought her head close to the keyhole. She applied the glue meticulously to the ignition lock, careful to outline just the keyhole so no glue would be visible. When it was done she sat back trembling in the driver seat, her heart pounding in her ears.

Wow, that was easier than I imagined, Elizabeth thought in relief. She caught Jessica's eye through the window and flashed her a thumbs-up signal. Jessica tried to return the gesture, but leaned her elbow on the horn of Mrs. Tracey's car, which let out a short blast.

Oh no! Elizabeth thought, staring at the Traceys' house in panic. She scrambled out of the car and darted toward Jessica. Jessica sprang into action at the same time, leaping out of her car and flipping the door shut. Bruce revved his engine and blew the bird whistle sharply.

"C'mon," Elizabeth urged, grabbing her sister's arm and pulling her across the wet lawn. They broke into a run and headed for the Porsche, slipping and skidding on the wet grass.

Bruce hastily opened the door as they arrived, panting and wet. They both dove into the passenger seat of the waiting Porsche, giddy with excitement. Bruce gunned the engine and turned swiftly onto the main road.

"Ohmigod, I'm soaking," said Jessica, laughing hysterically. "Elizabeth, would you get off my lap!"

"*You're* soaking! I'm drenched," said Elizabeth, tugging off the moist rubber gloves, which were sticking to her hands. She clambered into the backseat of the car.

Elizabeth's hair was dripping, and Jessica's scarf was plastered to her head. Jessica pulled it off and jammed it into the pocket of Bruce's raincoat. She shook out her hair wildly, spraying Bruce and Elizabeth.

"Jessica!" they both screamed.

"Oh, sorry!" she said, gasping with laughter as she pulled off her gloves finger by finger.

"Can you imagine," Elizabeth said, "when they try to start their cars—and—" She broke off, unable to finish her sentence because she was laughing so hard.

"And—and Mr. Tracey says, 'Jan, my car won't start. This is just *Krazy*,'" Jessica finished, wiping tears of laughter from her eyes.

"And Mrs. Tracey says, 'I know, it's a real Saab story,'" Bruce added, sending Jessica and Elizabeth into fits of hysterics. Suddenly they heard the sound of an alarm.

"Oh no, a siren!" Jessica cried.

"It's the police!" Bruce said, looking in the rearview mirror. A blue and white police car with its light flashing was rapidly approaching.

"Quick, hit the deck!" Jessica squealed. Jessica and Elizabeth dropped to the floor.

Bruce held his breath as the police car neared them. It came up quickly on his tail. Moving swiftly into the other lane to see what the police officer

74

would do, Bruce prayed he wouldn't stop. The police car zoomed by.

"A clean getaway!" said Bruce, letting out his breath.

"Yeess!" said Jessica, climbing back into her seat. "The sweet smell of success!" She raised her hand to Bruce for a high-five.

Bruce dropped off his partners in crime and returned to his house. He stepped into the elegant foyer of the Patman estate and shut the door quietly behind him. As he walked down the hall, his footsteps echoed eerily in the silent mansion.

He paused for a moment as he hung his raincoat in the closet next to his father's, his mood changing rapidly from exuberance to solemnity. "For the men in my life," his mother had said, beaming after she'd bought the matching Burberry raincoats and scarves for Bruce and his father. They had been on a family vacation together in London. Bruce smiled, remembering how she had sewed name tags on the coat labels because the two of them were always mixing up their clothes. Bruce had lost his scarf since, and Bruce and Roger—Bruce's cousin who lived with them—were now the only men that remained in Mrs. Patman's life.

Bruce shook his head and headed up the stairs, lost in thought. After London, they had gone to Scotland and Ireland. He remembered his parents posing next to the statue of Rodin's "The Kiss" at the wax museum in Dublin, and holding hands like teenagers as they wandered through Edinburgh. Bruce had been sullen for most of the trip, unhappy to be dragged around Europe with his parents. He regretted his attitude now.

He regretted a lot of things now, he realized as he got ready to go back to bed. There was only one person in the world who could make him feel better, and he had driven that person away.

After his girlfriend, Regina Morrow, had died, Bruce had thought he would never fall in love again. He had vowed never to have another relationship, never to make himself vulnerable again. Playing the field, dating all the girls he wanted without getting attached, had been his game plan for a long time. But when Pamela had come into his life, all that had changed. Pamela had softened him. She had made him open up again. He pictured her on the tennis courts, her graceful figure smoothly crossing the court as she returned a powerful backhand.

Bruce's eyes clouded over. He had never felt so alone in his life. Then he shook his head. There was no point in feeling sorry for himself. His parents were his top priority now. He needed all his energy to get his family back together.

Bruce lay in his bed in the silent Patman mansion, tossing and turning. *In just four hours, my parents will be together in the same room,* Bruce thought, his stomach tightening, thinking how high the stakes in Jessica's little game of sabotage actually were. His whole life hung in the balance.

Chapter 7

"Jessica, what in the world are you doing?" Lila exclaimed, eyeing her friend suspiciously on Wednesday morning.

Jessica was hopping around the girls' bathroom of Sweet Valley High with a safety pin in her mouth. She had one leg in a pair of cream-colored panty hose and was trying to balance herself as she pulled the other nylon leg up.

"Oh, hi, Li," Jessica said through clenched teeth. "Fancy meeting you here."

"Going somewhere?" Lila inquired.

"Darn!" Jessica exclaimed, letting the safety pin fall. She looked down in dismay as a long run traveled down her left leg. She ripped off the panty hose and threw them in the trash. "So, no stockings," she muttered.

"Nice undies," said Lila, looking with disdain at Jessica's white cotton underwear. Jessica was wearing a pair of days-of-the-week underpants that she wore only when she was at the very bottom of her under-wear pile. The word "Monday" was splashed across the front and back in bold red block letters.

"Do you mind?" Jessica asked, quickly pulling on a white cotton blouse and attaching an antique gold brooch to the neck. She then scrambled into a pleated, cream linen skirt and blazer she had "borrowed" from her mother's closet. The skirt promptly slipped to her hips.

"Hey, Li?" Jessica said, turning to face her friend, who was watching with her arms crossed. "You think you could give me a hand with this?" She took the safety pin out of her mouth and waved her hand at the oversize skirt.

"Yeah, yeah," Lila said, wondering when Jessica would deign to reveal the purpose behind her professional attire. "Turn around." Jessica turned around and faced the mirror, straightening the collar of her crisp white blouse.

"Ouch!" she screamed as the safety pin poked her sharply in the back.

"Jessica! If you keep fidgeting, I'm never going to be able to do this," Lila said.

"Sorry," Jessica said, forcing herself to stand still while Lila secured the safety pin. "Just try not to draw any more blood, OK?"

Lila watched as Jessica slipped her feet into a pair of low ivory heels. A pearl choker and a pair of understated gold earrings with pearl drops at the ends complemented the outfit.

Grabbing her cosmetic bag, Jessica turned toward the mirror to coat her lips in a sophisticated shade of mauve lipstick. She rubbed her lips with a tissue and smacked them together. Snatching a cream linen bow from her bag, she pulled her hair back at the nape of her neck for the final touch.

"Wow," she said out loud, gazing at herself in the mirror. "I look just like Mom!" Satisfied with the effect, she threw her regular clothes in her bag and turned to go.

"Jessica!" Lila demanded. "Where do you think you're going?" Lila was quickly losing patience with the way Jessica had been behaving lately, so secretive and sly.

"Oh, just some job interview for the summer," Jessica said finally in an offhanded tone.

"A *job* interview!" Lila said, horrified, raising her hands to her cheeks.

"Some of us have to work for a living," said Jessica breezily. "See you later!" She bolted out the door before Lila could follow.

Once in the hall, Jessica quickly looked around for any signs of teachers or administrators. She was supposed to be in study hall and didn't have a hall pass. Her heart pounding, she looked straight ahead and forced herself to walk slowly and deliberately, as if she had somewhere legitimate to go. She drew a deep breath as she took in the long corridor that stretched endlessly ahead of her.

"Ms. Wakefield!" a deep voice called from behind her. Jessica turned around quickly, her pulse racing. *Chrome Dome Cooper!* she thought in dismay. The principal was making his way quickly down the hall, his bald head glistening.

"Shouldn't you be in study hall?" asked Mr. Cooper when he'd reached her.

"Er, yes," Jessica said, thinking quickly. "But I have a *very* important job interview for the summer, and I could only get an appointment during the day."

Mr. Cooper gave her a dubious look.

"You see, Mr. Cooper," Jessica continued in a rush, "I think it's very important that I learn to take on more responsibility. It's part of a—a self-development program I'm on."

"I see. Do you have a note from home about this interview?" Mr. Cooper inquired.

"Uh, no, I don't," Jessica said. "I wanted this whole thing to be a surprise for my parents. . . . You won't tell them, will you?"

"No, Jessica," Mr. Cooper relented. "I won't tell them. I'll give you permission to miss study hall for your interview. But next time I won't be so lenient," he warned.

"Thanks, Mr. Cooper," Jessica said, flashing him a broad smile.

"And you keep up that self-development program," he called after her.

Bruce was pacing back and forth in the light misty drizzle falling over the school parking lot, waiting anxiously for Jessica. The rainstorm had done nothing to end the heat wave. *Why would it?* Bruce thought. *Why would anything happen to make my life easier?* He looked at his watch impatiently. They had only a half-hour study break, and it was already after nine.

Just then he noticed Pamela crossing the parking lot on her way to gym class. She was dressed in tennis whites and had her gym bag slung over her right shoulder.

"Pamela!" Bruce called, hurrying over to her.

"Hi, Bruce," Pamela said, her clear blue eyes cold and unwelcoming. She continued to walk briskly across the asphalt, her black hair christened with a few sprinkled raindrops.

Bruce fell into step beside her. "Do you think we could talk for a minute?" he asked.

Pamela stopped in her tracks. "What do you want, Bruce?" she asked, her jaw set. She had been heartbroken when she had realized that Bruce had fallen in love with Elizabeth Wakefield. When he'd actually left her for Elizabeth, she'd been totally humiliated. But she was determined not to let him know how hurt she was.

"Pamela—I'm sorry about what happened," Bruce said, swallowing hard. "I—I made a mistake. A huge mistake. I wasn't really in love with Elizabeth. I was just, uh, confused about my parents."

Pamela's eyes softened. She knew how difficult it was for Bruce to admit he was wrong. After Elizabeth and Todd had gotten back together, she had actually felt sorry for Bruce. She knew what a hard time he was going through, especially with his parents and all. She had even wanted to ask him how things were going with them, but had resisted the urge.

"Do you think we could have dinner sometime and talk about it?" Bruce asked carefully. "I—I miss you, Pamela."

Pamela hesitated. Her pride was still injured. But it would just be dinner, she thought. She should at least listen to what he had to say. She lifted her face toward his, opening her mouth to answer.

Suddenly Jessica emerged from the building.

"Hey, Bruce, you ready?" she called, hurrying toward him. Decked out in her mother's cream linen suit with matching low heels and a black leather briefcase, she looked like a young executive.

Pamela stared at the Wakefield twin in shock, taking in her business attire. *So Bruce really is still in love with Elizabeth,* Pamela thought. *They're spending every minute together.* "No, thank you, Bruce. I would not like to have dinner," she said in a frosty tone, trying to control the quaver in her voice. She turned her back on him and marched away.

"What's wrong, Brucie?" Jessica asked as she approached him. "Girl problems?"

Bruce turned on her in a rage. "Only if *you're* the girl," he growled.

"Hey, chill out," Jessica said lightly when she realized how upset he was.

"What took you so long?" Bruce demanded.

"Nothing. I just had to change," Jessica said, neglecting to tell him about her encounter with the principal. "So, do you have the goods?"

Bruce nodded, handing Jessica a large white shopping bag, damp from the rain. As soon as she grabbed the handles, the bottom of the bag fell out, and a square, gold album tumbled onto the asphalt. Jessica bent down quickly to retrieve it, dusting it off briskly with her hands.

"Would you be careful!" Bruce snapped. "That's my parents' wedding album."

"Since when are you so sentimental?" asked Jessica, annoyed.

"Since when are you so spastic?" returned Bruce. "What's your problem?"

"I told you," Jessica said indignantly, "during this phase of Mercury's orbit, everything goes haywire." Based on her experiences of the last few days, Jessica was now a firm believer in this theory.

"Well, it's certainly caused you to go haywire, Wakefield," said Bruce. "Do you think you can handle taking this up to the office, or do you need an escort to make sure you do it without falling on your face?"

Jessica shot Bruce a dirty look. She flipped open her mother's old briefcase, placed the album securely inside, and clicked it shut. She then made a quick about-face and walked haughtily to Bruce's Porsche. Just as she reached the car, she tripped and went sprawling against the passenger door. A low ivory heel went flying.

Jessica watched the shoe as it tumbled across the asphalt and rolled under a neighboring green Corvette. Suddenly she spotted Michael out of the corner of her eye, managing to look cooler than ever, despite the heat. He was slowly ambling across the parking lot to his Mazda. *It's uncanny,* she thought. *Every time I don't want to be seen, Michael Hampton makes an appearance.*

"Darnit, Jessica!" Bruce yelled as he ran to check the paint of his prized Porsche.

Feeling hot and muggy in her mother's suit, Jessica hobbled across the wet asphalt to retrieve her shoe, trying to appear as dignified as possible. "Shoot!" she exclaimed as she spotted it hiding behind a back tire. Wrapping her skirt around her body to prevent it from trailing in the gravel, she knelt down and reached under the car, feeling around blindly for the shoe. She finally made contact with it

83

and quickly pulled it out. Hopping lightly, she brushed off her bare foot and slipped it back into the shoe.

"Nice job, Wakefield," Bruce said as she joined him by the car. He was still meticulously inspecting the side of his Porsche for damage.

"Oh, I hope I didn't hurt your baby," Jessica said scornfully.

"You're lucky you didn't," Bruce responded.

"Call me Elizabeth!" she hissed to Bruce as she noticed Michael approaching his car.

"What?" Bruce asked.

"Just call me Elizabeth," Jessica repeated in an urgent whisper.

Bruce stared at her, perplexed.

"Oh, hi, Michael!" Jessica called, waving to him. "It's Elizabeth Wakefield, remember me?"

Just as Michael turned toward her, a gust of wind blew her skirt up to reveal her cotton days-of-the-week underwear with "Monday" plastered across the front in bright red letters. Jessica's face flamed to the roots of her golden-blond hair. *I think I'm going to die,* she thought. Mortified, she frantically smoothed down her skirt. *At least Michael thinks I'm Elizabeth,* she thought with some relief. She cast a sidelong glance at Bruce. Had he witnessed her humiliation?

"C'mon," Bruce said, practically pushing her into the car. *Good,* thought Jessica. *He didn't even notice.* She sat back in the cool, dry passenger seat, a dreamy smile on her face. She imagined the envious stares of her admiring friends as she and Michael strode slowly down the halls of Sweet Valley High, arm in arm, both wearing faded jean jackets. She thought with glee of the expression on Lila's face as she and Michael drove off in his red Mazda Miata, on their way to the latest Hollywood cast party or film screening.

Maybe she could land a role in Michael's father's film. Or at least make some connections. Maybe this was her big chance. As soon as Michael's father laid eyes on her, she would be on her way to stardom. And that would just be an added bonus to having Michael Hampton as her boyfriend.

"Hey, Jess?" Bruce asked, turning to her as he exited the highway and coasted into downtown Sweet Valley.

"Yes?" she answered, returning from her daydream.

"What happened? Did you slip into a coma?"

"I was just thinking," Jessica returned. "But I guess you don't know what that's like."

"Hmm," said Bruce, goading her on. "What were you thinking about, *Elizabeth*? Michael Hampton, perhaps?"

"So what if I was?" said Jessica huffily.

"Well, I hope *he* knows what day it is," Bruce said with a grin.

Blushing furiously, Jessica turned to him and pummeled him with her fists. "Shut up, Bruce!"

Bruce laughed and fended her off. As he continued to drive toward downtown, he seemed to be in a marginally better mood. "Now, are you sure you can handle this, Wakefield?" he asked as they pulled up across the street from the Traceys' office building, a modern steel and glass structure that looked clean and elegant.

"No problem. This will be a piece of cake," Jessica

said, jumping out of the car with her briefcase and smoothing her skirt. She hoped she was right. The towering structure loomed ahead of her forebodingly. As she stared at the building, her mother's words came back to her: "I mean it, no interfering in Bruce's parents' affairs."

Jessica took a deep breath and pushed through a set of swinging glass doors. She entered the air-conditioned lobby and looked around, carefully taking stock of her surroundings. There were two official-looking security guards sitting behind an imposing desk near the elevator bank.

Jessica tried to walk casually by the desk, but was stopped by one of the guards.

"Excuse me, miss!" he called.

"Yes?" She looked over her shoulder innocently.

"You got a building pass?" he asked.

"Oh, well, no," Jessica said, turning back to the desk. "I'm with Wakefield Interior Design," she said, trying to appear businesslike. "The Traceys are expecting me."

The security guard nodded and waved her on, handing her a green pass with an "8" stamped on it.

Once in the elevator, Jessica punched the button for the eighth floor and prepared her speech to the Traceys' secretary. "Hi, I'm Jessica Wakefield," she said out loud in a strong, composed voice. "I'm doing some work for my mother's design firm. We're redecorating the Traceys' offices, and I just need to take some quick measurements."

Then she would casually place the wedding album prominently on the coffee table in the reception area, where Mr. and Mrs. Patman wouldn't be able to miss it. They would have to browse through it while they waited futilely for the Traceys. Seeing pictures of their wedding would surely make them think twice about getting a divorce.

Shouldn't I be there already? Jessica wondered. She looked up and noticed a red light flashing. The panel at the top of the elevator indicated floor four. *It's not moving!* she thought in alarm. *Oh no, I'm stuck. There's something wrong with the elevator!* Panicked, she pressed the buttons for all the floors, then all the buttons randomly. "Help!" Jessica yelled, pounding on the elevator doors and cursing the planets above.

What is Jessica doing in there? thought Bruce, watching the building anxiously from his vantage point across the street. It seemed as though he had been saying that all week. She was going to make him late for his French class, and he was already in trouble with Ms. Dalton for not turning in his homework all last week.

Bruce drummed his fingers methodically against the steering wheel and glanced down at his watch. *Nine forty-five!* he thought in despair. His parents would be arriving any minute. Bruce couldn't imagine what could be keeping her. How long could it take to plant a book on a table? *I'd better go find her,* he thought grimly. He jumped out of the car and marched purposefully across the street.

Suddenly Bruce noticed his mother pull up in front of the building. And his father was right on her tail in his gray Cadillac. *Great!* Bruce thought to himself. He turned around and hightailed it back across

87

the street, ducking into his car and backing up rapidly into a side street so he couldn't be seen. *Please, Jessica,* he thought as he watched his parents walk together toward the shimmering building, *just come through this one time, just this one time.*

Jessica pushed the round of buttons again and pounded on the elevator door in vain. "Help! Help!" she yelled over and over, screaming until her throat was raw. But nobody seemed to hear. Finally she decided to take matters into her own hands. Bracing one shoulder against the wall, she wedged her manicured fingers between the rubber bumpers of the elevator doors. Then she pulled.

Nothing happened. She planted her feet more firmly and pulled again, gritting her teeth and grunting with the effort. Finally, sweat running down her back, she managed to separate the doors a few inches.

Anxiously she peered through the opening, then groaned loudly as she saw the concrete wall in front of her. She was between floors! The opening for the next floor was just above her head. *Maybe if I got the doors open enough,* she thought, *I could hoist myself up to the next floor.* She kicked off her heels and spaced her feet apart for more leverage. Then she squeezed her fingers between the elevator doors and forced them farther apart. Exerting all her strength, Jessica closed her eyes and pulled. But no matter how hard she pulled and pushed, the doors wouldn't open more than a few inches. Finally she let go, and the doors bounced back together. *Probably just as well,* she thought, remembering a horror story she'd heard about someone doing the same thing and falling down the elevator shaft to their death. *As if enough hasn't gone wrong this week.*

"But Bruce is going to kill me anyway," she said out loud. Her arms aching and her throat sore, she sighed and slid down the wall to the floor of the elevator. Crossing her legs and placing the wedding album on her lap, she opened it to the first page.

Wow, thought Jessica, sucking in her breath sharply. *They look just like movie stars!* Jessica gazed down at the blown-up color photo of the bride and groom on the first page. Mrs. Patman stared serenely out at the camera with her head held high, looking like a queen in her elaborate white wedding dress with its lace bodice, pinched waist, and full skirt. A garland of tiny baby's breath encircled the crown of her rich brown hair, and a long white veil flowed down her back and onto the floor. Mr. Patman stood next to her, smiling proudly, his hand resting lightly on his new wife's hip. He wore a classic black tuxedo with a thick silk cummerbund and a red rose in the breast pocket. *I can see why Mom fell in love with him in college,* Jessica thought as she studied the younger Mr. Patman. With his sculpted features, thick dark hair, and flashing green eyes, Mr. Patman looked just like Bruce. *They could be on the cover of* Bride & Groom *magazine,* thought Jessica with a dreamy sigh as she turned the page.

The next page revealed shots at the altar. Mr. and Mrs. Patman stood profiled in an ornate church as they took their vows and exchanged rings. Jessica turned forward a few pages to the reception. "Wow, they had such a traditional wedding," Jessica mur-

mured as she looked through the photos of the reception: The Patmans taking the first bite of the wedding cake, Mr. Patman removing Mrs. Patman's lace garter, Mrs. Patman throwing her bouquet to a crowd of young women with outstretched arms.

"No way am I going to have a wedding like that." Jessica's thoughts drifted away from the Patmans. In her mind, the purpose of a wedding was to get lots of attention and have lots of fun. She would have a simple ceremony on the beach, followed by a swinging party. All her friends would be there, and it would be the biggest bash of the century, thought Jessica in satisfaction. She pictured herself presiding over the event in a body-hugging, gold-sequined minidress with a matching bikini underneath, her hair swept dramatically up on her head, and long dangling earrings falling elegantly from her ears.

Jessica leaned back against the wall and continued to leaf through the reception pictures, coming to a long series of shots of various family members. Jessica flipped rapidly through the pages, getting bored with all the group photos and family shots. Then she turned to a blown-up close-up black-and-white shot of the Patmans kissing. *That's more like it,* Jessica thought as she gazed down at the page, enchanted by the magical image.

Finally Jessica reached the last pages of the album. The Patmans had changed out of wedding attire into honeymoon gear. Mr. Patman looked dapper in a light-blue seersucker suit, and Mrs. Patman looked slim and chic in a yellow knit dress with a matching bag. A small, round straw hat with a yellow ribbon was perched at an angle on her head. The last photo showed the couple getting into a vintage white Cadillac convertible with a "Just Married—Paris or Bust" banner on the back, a crowd of well-wishers throwing streamers and rice.

Jessica tried to imagine her mother in Mrs. Patman's place, standing elegantly with Hank Patman like royalty while their loyal subjects wished them well. Try as she might, she just couldn't envision it. She couldn't see her down-to-earth, radical mother standing by the side of stuffy, debonair Henry Wilson Patman III at the altar of a fancy church. A traditional pomp-and-circumstance wedding ceremony just wasn't her mother's style. It seemed so well suited for Mrs. Patman, though, Jessica mused. She seemed like the perfect mate for Mr. Patman.

Jessica closed the album and stared at it, lost in thought. The Patmans had clearly been so in love when they got married, with their whole lives ahead of them. *I wonder what went wrong?* Jessica thought. *Did they get bored with each other? Did their love fade?*

For the first time since she'd embarked on this quest with Elizabeth and Bruce, Jessica felt that her heart was in it. Hank and Marie Patman seemed like real people to her now. *There must be some way to make them feel the way they did when they got married,* Jessica reflected . . . *to bring them back to the past.* Jessica leaned against the cool elevator wall with the album on her lap, her mind clicking away at a hundred miles an hour.

Chapter 8

Marie Patman walked toward the Traceys' building at a fast clip, a strong, determined look on her face. This would be the first time she had seen her husband since she had moved out of the house, and she wasn't looking forward to it. She was determined to get through their meeting with as little contact as possible.

"Good morning, Marie," said Mr. Patman awkwardly as he caught up with his wife.

"Hello, Henry," replied Mrs. Patman coolly, dismayed that they had arrived at the same time.

Mr. Patman coughed uncomfortably. "Uh, quite a storm we had this morning."

"Yes," she said, wishing he wouldn't bother with the pleasantries.

"Too bad it didn't cool anything off," said Mr. Patman, feeling the air with his hand. "It's still as hot as the Sahara desert. At least it's clearing up now, though."

Mrs. Patman ignored him, hurrying toward the glass doors and opening them before he could do it for her. She couldn't believe that he was acting as if everything were normal. After she had moved out, Henry had made no move to get her back. He had agreed to go through the divorce proceedings without a struggle. Even though her husband hadn't admitted he was having an affair with Alice Wakefield, the fact that he had given up so easily on their marriage was proof enough for her.

Once inside, Mrs. Patman walked rapidly past the security guards and up to the elevator bank, pressing the call button of the elevator. Tensely wringing her hands together, she waited for it to come. Mr. Patman joined her, and they stood waiting in awkward silence for several minutes. He pushed the button again. Nothing.

"Looks like it's out of order," Mr. Patman finally said.

"Yes," replied Mrs. Patman. "I suppose we should inform the security guards."

"Excuse me," said Mr. Patman, making his way up to the security desk. "It appears the elevator is out of order."

"Yeah, we've been having trouble with these lifts all week," the security guard grumbled.

"We have a meeting in five minutes," said Mrs. Patman politely. "Do you think you'll have the elevator fixed in time?"

"No, ma'am, sorry to say, you're going to have to take the stairs." The security guard pointed toward the stairwell.

The Patmans turned in the direction indicated and trudged toward the stairs.

Mr. Patman lapsed into silence again as they made their way together up the steps. His wife seemed so unapproachable. He couldn't understand what had happened to make her so cold and remote. Everything had been fine, and then one day, out of the blue, she had accused him of having an affair with Alice Wakefield. *It's like she became a different person,* he thought. She used to be so gracious and accommodating. Then suddenly she had become nagging and suspicious, constantly questioning his every move.

Henry Patman had always led a high-pressured business life, flying off to meetings with important industry executives all over the world, and Marie had always supported him in his business endeavors. In fact, she was partly responsible for his success. She was a brilliant hostess whose refined manners and natural grace never failed to charm his clients. But then he had started doing business with Alice Wakefield, and his wife's attitude had totally changed. Marie had accused him both of neglecting her and of having an affair with another woman.

He'd felt as though he was being swept along on a tide of circumstances that he was incapable of stopping. *This is all her doing,* he thought in frustration as he plodded up the stairs behind her. She was the one who no longer had faith in him, in their marriage. She was the one who wanted the divorce.

Well, he thought stubbornly, *I guess I'll go through with it, because what's a marriage without trust?*

He looked up at his wife, marching methodically up the steps with her head held high. It hadn't always been like this, had it? He shook his head and continued to climb along with her, lost in thoughts of the past. The ascent up the eight flights of stairs felt like an eternity.

"Oh, you must be the Patmans!" the receptionist greeted them with a too-bright smile as they finally entered the Traceys' modern beige office, both a little out of breath.

Mrs. Patman heaved a sigh of relief, thankful to be out of the oppressive atmosphere of the stairwell, alone with her husband.

"That's right," she said, smiling in return. She paused to catch her breath. "Will you please tell Marty I've arrived?"

"The Traceys are running a little late this morning," the receptionist said, looking first at Marie, then at Hank Patman. "It seems they've had some car trouble. If you would just have a seat . . ."

Mrs. Patman sighed and headed into the waiting area, her soon-to-be ex-husband following close behind.

Mr. Patman took off his raincoat and turned to help his wife out of hers, but she was already hanging her coat on the coatrack. He grimaced and hung his coat up next to hers. They sat down together in a set of plush green chairs in the corner of the waiting room. Mrs. Patman picked up a copy of *Better Homes and Gardens*, opened it randomly, and began to read. Mr. Patman followed her lead, grabbing a copy of *Newsweek* off the glass coffee table and turning to the feature story.

They sat quietly together, the silence interrupted only by sounds of pages turning. Mr. Patman couldn't concentrate. He gazed down at the page, the words blurring in front of him. The wall clock sat across from him, its second hand rotating slowly around the face. The wait seemed interminable. He'd never felt so powerless in his life.

Mrs. Patman stared at a picture of the interior of a beach house in Malibu. The spread depicted a happy young couple lounging in a living room decorated like a tropical paradise. The picture made her heart constrict, and she slammed the magazine shut. Her foot tapping impatiently, she wished the Traceys would appear. She didn't know how much longer she could endure being in the same room with her husband. Finally she broke the silence, unable to bear the tension in the air. "Well, it seems that everything that can go wrong, will," she said, looking at her watch, annoyed. "It poured this morning, the elevator is broken, the Traceys are late. . . . I'm surprised the electricity is still working."

As soon as the words were out of her mouth, Mrs. Patman regretted them. She had unwittingly made a reference to their honeymoon in Paris, when the electricity in their hotel room had been out for most of the week. Despite terrible weather and every sort of mishap possible, the trip had been a romantic and unforgettable experience.

Mrs. Patman looked away, hoping her remark would go unnoticed, but Mr. Patman picked up on it. "You know, that reminds me of—" he began.

Suddenly there was a sharp pop and the lights in the waiting room went out.

Mr. and Mrs. Patman both jumped in surprise, then started chuckling in spite of themselves.

"Oh, dear!" exclaimed the receptionist. "I'm so

sorry! I'll be back in a second." She jumped up and went in search of the fuse box.

". . . of Paris, when there was no electricity in our hotel room," finished Mr. Patman, laughing softly.

"Or in most of the city, for that matter," added Mrs. Patman. She closed her mouth quickly, sorry that she had engaged in a conversation with her husband.

Henry Patman's eyes were slowly adjusting to the dim light in the room. He watched as his wife fidgeted with the handle of her handbag. The gesture, combined with the sudden memory of their Parisian honeymoon, filled him with unexpected tenderness.

"Marie, remember when we ate by candlelight in that Greek restaurant in the Latin Quarter?" he ventured tentatively.

"That was so romantic," she said wistfully, thinking back to the evening. She remembered sitting across from Henry in the intimate French restaurant, swept away with emotion. Quite a contrast to the last few years, when they had eaten at opposite ends of a long dining table, barely able to see each other. And that was on the nights he was home. Usually she, Bruce, and Roger ate alone in the kitchen while Henry stayed at work. Mrs. Patman's thoughts returned to the past, when she and Henry had gallivanted around Paris like enchanted teenagers. Their honeymoon had been such a magical experience.

"Until our waiter started dropping everyone's orders!" Mr. Patman added.

"That's right," said Mrs. Patman, transported to the past. "It was so dark that you stepped on a dish of moussaka on our way out of the restaurant."

"Yeah, everything was on strike that week," Mr.

Patman recalled. "Electricity, trains, metro . . ."

"We had to walk all the way across the Seine in the pouring rain to get to the Louvre," Mrs. Patman remembered.

"And it was closed because of the blackout!" added Mr. Patman.

"Oh, Henry," said Mrs. Patman, reminiscing, "you were so disappointed."

"So you took me to an old movie theater to cheer me up."

"But the movie was in French, and we couldn't understand a word!"

"That's right," Hank Patman said. "We just sat in the balcony, giggling together, trying to fill in the dialogue."

"When we left, the sun was shining, and the streets of Paris were glittering." Marie Patman looked wistful.

"Remember our picnic in the Luxembourg gardens?" said Mr. Patman, gazing at his wife.

"Our picnic!" said Mrs. Patman. "I had forgotten about our picnic! We spent the whole morning shopping on St. Michel—we found a little blue blanket, and candles, and what else, Hank?"

"Red wine and cheese and bread," he said.

"Right, but then didn't it start pouring again?" she asked.

"Yeah, we ducked into a patisserie to get out of the rain. . . . But unfortunately, I already had a baguette in my hand," he recalled.

"The owner thought you stole it!" said Mrs. Patman.

"And we just ran!" said Mr. Patman.

"Oh, Henry," said Mrs. Patman said, gasping with laughter, "the image of you running down St. Michel

with that soaked baguette in your hand while this little French man chased you, screaming, 'Monsieur,
monsieur, arrêtez, arrêtez!' It's just too much." She
wiped tears of laughter from her eyes.

"That was the best baguette I ever ate," said Mr.
Patman softly.

They were silent for a moment, lost in memories
of the past. Mr. Patman looked tenderly through the
dim light at his wife. Her eyes were sparkling and her
cheeks were flushed. *This is the woman I married,* he
thought, suddenly awash in new love for his wife.
This is the woman I wanted to spend my life with.

The electricity suddenly came back on, bringing
them back abruptly to the harsh reality of the present. The bright, artificial lights of the sterile law office provided a startling contrast to their hazy
memories of Paris.

"Sorry about that!" the receptionist said cheerfully, popping back into the waiting area. "It appears
we had some kind of electrical short. Something to
do with the elevator. Everything's in order now."

Mr. Patman looked over at his wife, and was startled to see her sitting up straight with her lips tightly
pursed. He tugged at his tie and turned away uncomfortably. Well, that moment had certainly passed. Just
like that time in their lives had passed. What had
happened to change everything? he wondered. When
they had gotten married they had vowed that their
whole life together would be one long honeymoon.
When had the honeymoon ended?

He tried to think back to the last time they had
spent any real time together, just the two of them. He
couldn't come up with anything. They were like

strangers passing in the night now. He was up at dawn, at breakfast with the paper, at work until all hours, and then home for dinner. That is, if he wasn't out of town for business. He shook his head. He really had been working hard lately—well, actually, in the last few years. But hadn't he done it all for her, to provide her with a beautiful home and security?

Mr. Patman shook his head. He wasn't being honest with himself. He knew he couldn't buy his wife happiness. He had been taking her for granted for years, secure in the knowledge that she would be there when he left in the morning and waiting for him when he got home at night. Yes, this was all his fault. With all the time he spent away, and the meager amount of attention he gave her, who could blame her for being suspicious?

Mr. Patman was filled with a new sense of purpose. He wanted his wife back. He wanted the sparkling, vibrant woman he loved back. He wasn't going to let his pride ruin his marriage.

"Marie." He turned to her with urgency in his voice. "What I had with Alice Wakefield is ancient history, and ancient history only. We were kids. She never meant, or could mean, what you mean to me."

"But I thought—" Marie began, confused.

"I know what you thought, and I didn't do anything to discourage you. I don't blame you for having suspicions," Mr. Patman said. "But it's not another woman that has come between us—it's my work. And that's going to change."

"Hank, slow down, please. This is too much to digest right now," said Mrs. Patman, wanting badly to believe him.

"Let's go have breakfast," said Mr. Patman with newfound vigor, feeling younger than he had in years. "God only knows what happened to the Traceys, and frankly, I don't care."

An irresistible smile began to play on Marie's lips.

"Come on, let's go to our favorite place for brunch," Mr. Patman said, taking her hands between his. "The Ocean Terrace." The Ocean Terrace was a popular seaside restaurant renowned for its fresh seafood dishes and its banquet-style brunch. When they had first gotten married, the Patmans had gone there every Sunday morning. But, like so many other rituals, it had fallen by the wayside.

"All right, all right," said Mrs. Patman finally, laughing in between tears.

They gathered their coats and headed back toward the reception area. Mr. Patman held out Mrs. Patman's coat cautiously. She smiled as she slipped her arms into the sleeves. The receptionist looked at them, troubled. "I'm terribly sorry about the delay," she said, "but the Traceys should be here any minute. They called about ten minutes ago and said they were hopping into a cab."

"Quite all right," said Mr. Patman jovially. "In fact, I don't think we'll be needing their services any longer." He looked at Marie for confirmation.

"That's right," said Marie, her eyes sparkling. "Would you just leave them a message to that effect?"

"Of course, Mrs. Patman," replied the receptionist, smiling.

"Do you still have the scarf that goes with that coat?" Mrs. Patman asked her husband with a sentimental smile as they turned to go.

"I keep it right here in the pocket!" Mr. Patman said proudly, reaching in and pulling out a pink chiffon scarf with "Alice" written all over it.

Mrs. Patman stared in horror at Alice Wakefield's scarf. *To think I actually believed him! How could I have been so naive? How could I have actually swallowed his story that he had been busy with work and not another woman? That was the oldest line in the book! How could I have allowed myself to get swept away so easily into the past and to forget about the ugly reality of the present?*

She turned on her heel and ran from the room. Just as she got to the elevator, the doors opened and she found herself face-to-face with one of the Wakefield twins—looking all too much like her mother. Mrs. Patman felt as though she were going crazy, experiencing an onslaught of Alice Wakefields. She gasped and ran for the stairs.

Jessica watched in alarm as first Mrs. Patman headed for the stairs, looking as if she'd seen a ghost, and then Mr. Patman came running after her, waving Alice Wakefield's pink scarf.

"Marie! Marie!" he yelled. "It's not what you think!"

"Don't even bother," said Bruce in disgust as Jessica came out to the car, sheepishly holding the wedding album and trying to explain what had happened. He had just seen his mother run out the door in tears and get into her car. She had slammed the door, gunned the engine, and sped away, practically running down his father in the process. For some reason, his father had been waving a pink chiffon scarf.

Bruce sighed. Back to square one.

Chapter 9

Elizabeth sat alone with her journal in the cool Wakefield kitchen early Thursday morning, lost in thought about the Patman situation. Her black mood was at odds with the bright California sunshine pouring into the room. A cold cup of coffee sat untouched in front of her.

After the fiasco of Plan Two, Elizabeth was beginning to doubt their ability to get Bruce's parents back together. The Patmans' impending divorce proceedings loomed nearer with each passing day. It seemed as though all their efforts had only succeeded in pushing Mr. and Mrs. Patman further apart. *Maybe Jessica was right after all about this Mercury-in-retrograde stuff,* Elizabeth thought, starting to feel desperate. *We have just got to get Bruce's parents back together.* She was beginning to realize that her interest in the Patmans was not entirely altruistic. She needed the Patmans to get back together to reassure herself that her little fling with Bruce had been just that: a fling.

Elizabeth opened her journal to an empty page. She wanted to sort out her feelings, and it always helped to get her thoughts down on paper. Elizabeth hesitated for a moment, biting thoughtfully on the edge of her pen. Then she leaned over her composition book and began to write.

"Todd can't understand why I want to help Bruce so much. I've explained to him that Bruce is my friend and that I know what he's going through. Todd acts like he understands, but I know he's still sort of baffled. I guess I'm not being completely honest with him. But how can I tell him that I need to know once and for all that Bruce and I aren't meant to be together? That the parallels between my relationship with Bruce and Mom's romance with Mr. Patman make me uncertain? After everything that happened, how can I tell him that I'm still plagued with doubt?

"Everyone always says that I'm a carbon copy of Mom," Elizabeth continued steadily. "Sometimes I wish I had lived in the sixties, like her. Everything seemed so idealistic then—peace and love and all that . . . bell-bottoms, long hair, love beads, peace signs. Mom was so radical at college, always taking part in campus sit-ins and protest marches. I guess I'm a lot like her—concerned with social issues."

Elizabeth paused, thinking back to her own attempts to establish social justice. She had recently printed a controversial article about sexual harassment in *The Oracle*, despite administrative restrictions, and she had organized a Jungle Prom to promote environmental awareness. She bent her head and continued to write, the words pouring forth in a rush.

"And Bruce is just like his father—rich, conservative—*ultra*conservative. I can just see Mr. Patman at college, sitting in a plush lounge with his fraternity brothers, a cigar in his mouth and a whiskey in his hand."

Elizabeth paused for a moment to reflect. The image of her mother and Mr. Patman stood out vividly in her mind. She picked up her mug and took a sip, oblivious to the bitter taste of the cold coffee.

"How is it possible for two people who are so different to have fallen in love?" Elizabeth wrote, her pen scratching rapidly across the page. "To have fallen in love and gotten engaged? I guess it's true that opposites attract—how else can I explain my attraction to Bruce last week? Well, if it's true that Mr. and Mrs. Patman really *do* belong together, then Bruce and I definitely *don't* belong together. After all, I belong with Todd, don't I?"

Elizabeth closed her journal with a snap and stared down at the black and white composition book, the final words echoing in her mind: *I belong with Todd, don't I? I belong with Todd, don't I?*

Suddenly Elizabeth's reverie was broken by the sound of Jessica thumping down the stairs.

"Why didn't you wake me?" Jessica demanded as she careened into the kitchen.

"I didn't realize I was your alarm clock," Elizabeth retorted.

"Mine didn't go off," Jessica said in a panic.

Elizabeth glanced down at her watch. It looked as if Jessica was going to make her late for school again.

"I just can't understand it. That's the third time

this week that my alarm hasn't gone off," Jessica said, shaking her head.

"Maybe you should try setting it," Elizabeth suggested mischievously.

"Thanks for the tip, Liz," Jessica said, grabbing a container of yogurt and ripping it open.

"What were you doing up till all hours in the morning, anyway?" Elizabeth asked, yawning. The faint noises coming from Jessica's room had kept her up for hours.

"I was up until four trying to retrieve my history term paper on your old computer. I tried to recall it, but there was nothing there. Five whole pages, *hours* of senseless labor," Jessica lamented.

"Did you save it?" asked Elizabeth.

"Of course I saved it!" Jessica said indignantly, quickly spooning down yogurt. "It's this Mercury-in-retrograde thing. How could Mr. Jaworski assign a paper when the planets are going nuts?"

"There's no justice," Elizabeth agreed tolerantly.

"How am I ever going to explain this to him?" Jessica wailed, dumping her empty yogurt into the sink.

"Just tell him that the planets aren't aligned," Elizabeth suggested. "I'm sure he'll understand."

Jessica threw her arms up in frustration. "You have no respect for the order of the universe."

"Well, Jess, order or no order, time moves on, and you've got fifteen minutes before school starts," Elizabeth said.

With that, Jessica catapulted up the stairs. Elizabeth listened with amusement to the sounds of Jessica charging around madly as she jumped in the shower, dressed furiously, and threw her books together. Suddenly Elizabeth heard a small explosion, followed by Jessica's sharp scream.

Oh no! Elizabeth thought. She ran quickly up the stairs to find a distraught Jessica holding up a smoking blow-dryer.

"Can anything else go wrong?" Jessica cried.

"C'mon, Jess," Elizabeth said, taking her sister by the shoulders and marching her down the steps. "Let's get you out of the house before you blow the whole place up."

Elizabeth led her firmly out the back door to the garage, where the Jeep was parked.

"Oh, Elizabeth?" Jessica said. "Do you think I could borrow your keys? I can't find mine anywhere."

"You think I'm going to let you drive?" Elizabeth said incredulously as she headed for the driver's side of the Jeep.

Jessica turned sharply into an empty parking spot at Sweet Valley High and pulled the Jeep to a screeching halt. The car lurched forward, and Elizabeth flew back against the passenger seat, wondering how she had let Jessica talk her into driving to school.

"Jessica, just because we're going to be late doesn't mean you have to risk our lives," Elizabeth said in a piqued tone.

"Liz, I'm sorry!" Jessica exclaimed. "It's just that I've been late every day this week. Yesterday I missed French class entirely, and Ms. Dalton is going to *kill* me—"

Elizabeth got out of the car before Jessica could

finish, rolling her eyes. She couldn't wait for Mercury to go out of retrograde, or whatever it did that would make Jessica get her act together—or at least as together as she ever got it. Being around her sister when the planets were out of alignment was getting to be both exhausting and dangerous, judging from this morning's blow-dryer incident.

Jessica jumped out of the car and ran after her, trying to smooth her hair with her hands. "Oh, my hair," she moaned. "With this heat, if I don't blow-dry it, it's totally frizzy. I'll just have to put it up, I guess. Can you hold this?" She handed her book bag to Elizabeth, then scrabbled in her purse for a pen.

Elizabeth waited impatiently as Jessica scooped her blond hair up, twisted into a tight ponytail, then turned the ponytail back on itself to make a tight bun. Taking the pen from her mouth, she stuck it expertly through the knot. It stayed in place.

"There. It looks gross, but it'll have to do. As soon as Mercury rises, I'll be able to deal with my appearance more," she said confidently. She took her book bag back from Liz and headed toward school at a brisk pace.

"Jessica, when you're late, I'm late too. From now on, if you can't make it to school on time, you're just going to have to get a ride with someone else— Mercury or no Mercury," Elizabeth said sternly, walking quickly beside her sister.

"Liz, I said I was sorry," Jessica said cajolingly. "I had the worst morning in the history of the world— my whole life is falling apart. If I don't get the Patmans back together, Bruce will kill me, and I'll be ruined forever with Michael Hampton. Please don't be mad—it would really send me over the edge."

Elizabeth could never stay mad at Jessica for long. "No, I'm not mad at you," she said, her face softening. "I'm just mad that we're late for class again, that's all."

"I promise it'll never, never happen again!" Jessica vowed.

"Jess, that's one promise you'll never be able to keep," Elizabeth retorted.

The twins rushed through the front doors of school and sprinted down the hall together to their lockers. Jessica looked around when she got to her locker, relieved to see that the corridor was entirely deserted. She was hoping to avoid everybody she knew until she looked more presentable. "Do you think I have time to run to the bathroom to straighten up?" Jessica asked her sister.

"If you don't mind missing English class," Elizabeth responded, looking up at the big round clock on the wall. They were ten minutes late for class, and the morning announcements had already begun.

"Chrome Dome Cooper's in fine form this morning," said Jessica, listening as the principal rattled on over the PA system about litter in the hallways. "I mean, you'd think he'd find something more interesting to—"

Suddenly Jessica stopped in midsentence as she noticed Michael at the water fountain. *Ohmigod, I'm a total disaster,* Jessica thought in horror. *My hair's in this awful bun, my makeup is a mess, and I have raccoon eyes.* Michael turned away from the water fountain and began walking toward them.

Just as he passed by, Jessica turned to Elizabeth,

111

who was taking her morning books from her locker. "Bye, Jessica!" she exclaimed brightly. She pivoted quickly and ran off to class.

Elizabeth slammed her locker shut and stared after Jessica in amazement. *Had she heard correctly? Was her sister losing her mind?*

"It was a complete nightmare," said Lila, recounting her date with the new tennis pro, Jason Wynter, in the lunchroom. Jessica, Amy, Jeannie, and Maria were huddled around her, eager to hear all the details.

"You're kidding!" exclaimed Amy excitedly. "I thought you two would be perfect for each other!"

"Bad karma," Lila said, waving a hand dismissively.

"Where did you go?" asked Maria.

"To Pedro's, of all places. I mean, can you believe?" Lila said. Pedro's was a small Mexican restaurant in San Farando, a nearby town.

"I love Pedro's," Jessica interjected, thinking what an impossible snob Lila was. "My family goes there all the time."

"Well, so do I. But, I mean, Mexican food for a first date? Chips and burritos and rice?" Lila scoffed.

"So, what did you talk about?" asked Jeannie.

"What did we talk about? We talked about Jason Wynter, that's what," Lila said in a disgusted tone. "He just went on and on about himself for hours—his car, his tennis, his money. I couldn't get a word in."

"I can see why you didn't like him," said Jessica, smiling slyly. It would be torture for Lila not to be able to talk about herself.

"What an utter bore," said Lila disdainfully. "I've never met anyone so pretentious and self-centered in my life."

"Hmm, he sounds a lot like someone I know," Jessica said playfully, looking straight at Lila.

"Well, at least I've got something to be self-centered about," Lila said huffily, tossing her hair over her shoulder. "He was a total loser."

"But a gorgeous loser! Did he kiss you good night?" asked Amy eagerly, pressing for details.

"Kiss me good night? Are you kidding? I wouldn't let him near me!" Lila said haughtily.

Amy looked disappointed.

"Well, it doesn't sound like you two were destined to be together," put in Jeannie. "No cosmic attraction of opposites."

"Yeah, I think it's time to set my sights on another victim," Lila said, rubbing her hands together, her brown eyes gleaming.

"And who might that be?" Jessica asked.

"Oh, you know," said Lila pointedly. "Just another poor defenseless senior."

"Wow, Lila, you sure are on a manhunt this week," Amy said.

"Well, the horoscope hotline said aggressive behavior is the key to luck in love for Leos," said Lila. "So if I want to land the latest senior, this may be my last chance."

"That is, if I don't get there first," Jessica said. She combed the crowded cafeteria with a practiced eye, looking for signs of Michael. Now that her hair was dry and fluffed around her shoulders, her makeup reapplied, and her composure regained, she was anx-

113

ious to make it clear to Michael who Jessica Wakefield really was.

"You think you can compete with me, Jessica?" said Lila, her eyebrows raised.

"Of course not, Li. It's no competition!" Jessica answered coolly. Her eyes finally lit upon Michael sitting alone at a corner table. His head was hunched over a notebook, and he was scribbling furiously.

"See ya later, guys," said Jessica, gathering up her books and abruptly ditching her friends. She strolled through the noisy lunchroom nonchalantly, making her way casually to Michael's table. When he looked up in surprise, she gave him one of her famous Wakefield smiles and sat down.

"Hi, Michael," Jessica said. "You look like you could use some company."

"Hi, Jessica, how are you?" asked Michael in a flat voice. He quickly shut his notebook.

"Fabulous," she said, brushing her hair back off her shoulders lightly. "And you?" She looked him straight in the eye.

"Oh, all right," Michael said, looking away self-consciously.

"I'm just *too* busy these days, though," Jessica said, crossing her legs and leaning back. "With cheerleading and Pi Beta Alpha and my acting—I just feel like I'm being pulled in all directions. But that's the way it is, you know . . ."

"Uh-huh," grunted Michael.

"Not that I don't have time to go out," Jessica added.

Michael coughed slightly. "Actually, Jessica, I've been meaning to ask you . . ."

114

"Yes?" Jessica breathed excitedly.

"Uh, your sister, the, um, awkward one—" he began.

"I've got only one sister!" Jessica piped in merrily.

"Right," said Michael. "Uh, what's she into, your sister?"

"Elizabeth? Not much of anything, really," Jessica answered, warning bells going off in her head. If Michael found out about Elizabeth's work at *The Oracle* . . . "Poor dear—she pretty much studies all the time. Actually, she's really square—a straight-A student. It's unbelievable—Elizabeth is always stuck in front of some textbook. I try to make her get out more, but, well—" Jessica shrugged her shoulders.

Michael nodded, digesting the information thoughtfully.

"But why do you ask?" Jessica asked in a seemingly unconcerned tone.

"Oh, no reason in particular," said Michael. "It's just that I saw her dressed up in a suit, so I thought she might have a part-time job or something. . . ."

"Oh, that!" said Jessica, eager to play up the moment. "She had a job interview for the summer. Poor thing. I think she isn't used to walking in heels."

"Oh," said Michael, suppressing a smile.

"So, working on a play?" asked Jessica, anxious to turn the conversation away from her sister. "Maybe I could act out some of the scenes for you."

"Oh no—this is nothing. Just my private thoughts, really."

"Oh," said Jessica, looking at his journal longingly. She was burning with curiosity to read it. What had he written about her? she wondered. Jessica imagined the first entry: "Just met the most beautiful, fascinating girl. She's cultured, suave, sophisticated, the girl of my dreams. . . ."

"Well," said Michael, breaking into her reverie abruptly, "I've gotta run." He picked up his books and stood. "Take care of your sister!" he added cryptically as he turned to go.

Hmm, thought Jessica, completely captivated. *He must be playing hard to get.* If she was interested before, now she was *hooked.*

"OK, if I come with you to *The Oracle* now for fifteen minutes, and then you meet me after my afternoon practice," said Todd, calculating, "we'll have a total of one hour together today!"

Todd and Elizabeth were on their way to the newspaper office after school. Elizabeth had to add the finishing touches to her weekly "Personal Profiles" column before the paper went to press.

"Well, I guess that's better than yesterday," said Elizabeth. "But Todd, if we spend all our time together talking about our time together . . ."

"Then we're not really spending any time together," Todd finished, nodding.

"Right," said Elizabeth, smiling.

Todd stopped at a set of lockers to stretch out a hamstring. "The coach is really running us ragged," he said. "Yesterday we did twenty minutes of lay-up lines, then we scrimmaged for an hour and did a half-hour of three-on-two full-court fast-break drills."

"Wow," said Elizabeth, "sounds like he's really giving you a workout."

"And that was just the afternoon," Todd said. "In

evening practice, we had to do an hour of drills and run a full-court press. Then, to top it all off, we had to do suicides, wind sprints, and full-court lay-up lines at the end of practice."

"You're really going to be in great shape for the rest of the season," Elizabeth said.

"Yeah, that's for sure," Todd said, taking her hand. "If I can make it that far."

As they turned the corner of the hall together, Elizabeth felt a pair of eyes boring into her. She turned to catch Michael Hampton quickly averting his gaze. Elizabeth continued walking, completely perplexed. It seemed wherever she was, Michael was staring at her with that intense expression in his eyes. In the cafeteria, in French class, in study hall. It really seemed as though he was interested in her, but he never approached her. After all, she was almost always with Todd. It was obvious that she and Todd were boyfriend and girlfriend. So what was the deal?

Chapter 10

"So, did you hear about the beach barbecue tonight?" Lila asked as she accompanied Jessica to her locker on the way to lunch on Friday.

"What beach barbecue?" Jessica asked.

"Winston and Maria decided in homeroom today to throw a Bring-Your-Own-Burger barbecue for the entire junior class tonight," explained Lila. "But I guess you won't be able to make it, because you're grounded."

Jessica shrugged her shoulders, annoyed at Lila's overly sympathetic tone. "Oh, well. If you've been to one beach party, you've been to them all," she said lightly, determined not to let Lila know she was disappointed.

"But you haven't been to one like this," Lila said.

"Why not?" Jessica asked. "What's so special about this party?"

"Well, guess who's going to be there?" Lila asked tantalizingly.

"I don't know. Who?" asked Jessica, getting tired of her friend's game.

"Michael Hampton, that's who," said Lila victoriously.

"Why in the world would Michael Hampton go to a junior-class barbecue?" Jessica asked.

"Because I'm going to ask him to, that's why," Lila declared. "At lunch today. I'm going to just— Hey, looks like you've got an admirer, Jess," she said, interrupting herself.

"Where?" Jessica looked around wildly. Lila pointed to Jessica's locker. Leaning against the locker was a huge bouquet of brightly colored spring flowers.

"Flowers! Who are they from?" Jessica exclaimed, knowing exactly who: Michael Hampton. *It would be just like him to make a sophisticated gesture like this,* she thought. *Self-assured guys always act like this. They play it cool, they act uninterested, and then they go in for the kill.*

"You sure you want to ask Michael out when he's sending *me* flowers?" Jessica asked slyly, picking up the card. She began slitting open the envelope, then noticed it was addressed to Elizabeth. She dropped the card as if she were burned.

"It's for Elizabeth," she said in disgust.

"Oh, what a shame," said Lila, a triumphant smile playing on her lips. "What are the flowers doing in front of your locker, then?"

"I have no idea," Jessica replied, picking the card up off the ground.

"Well, aren't you going to open it?" Lila demanded, her hands on her hips.

Jessica looked at the card, considering. Why

shouldn't she open it? After all, the flowers were in front of *her* locker, weren't they? Then she reconsidered, remembering how angry Elizabeth had been the last time she had intercepted a letter from Todd.

"Of course not," Jessica said self-righteously. "I don't open my sister's mail."

"Since when?" Lila asked.

"Humph," Jessica returned, looking at the flowers and groaning. "Now I suppose I've gotta go find Liz and give her her stupid flowers before they die," she complained. "She's probably hiding out at the *Oracle* office, trying to be unsociable. I'll meet you at lunch, OK?"

"See ya," said Lila, sauntering off.

"Oh, and Li," said Jessica, calling after her. Lila stopped and turned. "Try not to be *too* aggressive. You wouldn't want to scare him off."

"Don't worry about it," said Lila smugly, waving and walking away.

Jessica sighed and headed grudgingly to the *Oracle* office to deliver the flowers to her sister. "So now I'm Elizabeth's personal delivery girl," she muttered as she made her way up the stairs and down the hall. Still grumbling, she pushed open the door to the newspaper office. Striding in, she tripped on a typewriter cord, sending her books, the flowers, and the card flying. Jessica landed sprawling at Elizabeth's feet.

"Oh, hi, Jess," said Elizabeth. "Making another dramatic entrance, I see."

"Some sympathy," Jessica snapped, picking herself up and dusting herself off. When was this Mercury-in-retrograde business going to be over? she wondered. She didn't know how much longer she could take it.

121

"Gee, Jess," said Elizabeth, picking up Jessica's latest book, *The Sun, the Stars, and You*. "I've never seen you take such an interest in literature."

"I can't believe it," Jessica said hotly, punctuating her words. "Here I am *personally* delivering flowers from your *sickeningly* sweet boyfriend and missing out on *precious* gossip in the lunchroom—and this is the thanks I get."

"I'm sorry, Jessica." Elizabeth smiled. "Thanks." She put the card and flowers on her desk and picked up the newspaper column in front of her.

"What are you working on?" Jessica asked, looking over her sister's shoulder.

"Oh, I'm just proofing this week's 'Personal Profiles' column. We're going to press this afternoon," Elizabeth said.

"Nice flowers, huh?" Jessica asked.

"They are nice," agreed Elizabeth, smelling the bouquet. "My favorite spring colors—yellow, pink, and orange."

"What do you think the card says?" Jessica persisted.

"Oh, I don't know," Elizabeth said, turning back to her work. "I guess I'll read it later."

Jessica stared at her sister's back. Elizabeth clearly had no intention of reading the card in front of her. *As if I'm interested in watching her coo like some dumb lovebird while she reads a boring love letter from stuffy Todd Wilkins*, Jessica thought huffily. She turned and carefully stormed out of the office, watching her feet.

Elizabeth watched her leave, an amused expression on her face. Then she sat back at her desk and quickly ripped open the card. Her eyebrows knit in puzzlement when she saw the unfamiliar signature scrawled at the bottom. *Michael Hampton!* she thought in surprise. *Dear Elizabeth,* she read silently,

> *I never dreamed or hoped I'd see,*
> *A girl like you who trips like me.*
> *You're beautiful and clumsy, too,*
> *You're just my secret dream come true.*
> *I'll see your face where e'er I roam,*
> *Won't you please let me drive you home?*

Elizabeth stared at the card, perplexed. Clumsy? Suddenly everything became clear—Jessica's strange behavior after the incident with her locker, Jessica's bizarre exit that morning in the hall. And, knowing Jessica, that was probably just scratching the surface. *So that's why Jessica's been passing herself off as me,* Elizabeth thought with a wry frown. *So she can make a good impression on Michael Hampton. He thinks I'm the one who's been acting like a total klutz.*

Elizabeth's spark of anger quickly faded as a mischievous idea popped into her head. *Well, two can play at that game,* she thought with a glint in her eye. *Maybe the Patmans aren't the only ones who need some assistance with their love life. Maybe my darling sister needs a little matchmaking as well.*

Elizabeth scanned her column a final time, her sharp eyes searching rapidly for grammatical errors and missed typos. She glanced down at her watch, hoping she would have time to talk to Todd before lunch period ended. She and Todd had planned to sneak in a quick ice-cream soda together at Casey's after school before his afternoon basketball practice. Elizabeth hated to cancel their plans, but it looked as if she didn't have a choice.

"Here, Penny, it's all set," Elizabeth said, handing the proofed copy to Penny Ayala, the editor of *The Oracle*.

"Thanks, Liz," said Penny, smiling.

"See you later," Elizabeth said, throwing her canvas book bag over her shoulder and hurrying out of the office. She rushed down the hall to the cafeteria, hoping she wouldn't be too late to catch Todd. Scanning the cafeteria quickly, she was relieved to find Todd sitting at a long table with a group of friends from the basketball team.

"Liz!" Todd exclaimed, his eyes lighting up. "I thought you'd be all wrapped up at the newspaper." He pulled her down to him for a quick hug.

"I just finished," Elizabeth explained breathlessly, untangling herself from Todd's arms. "But Todd, about this afternoon . . ." She hesitated and lowered her voice, drawing him close to her. Quickly she filled him in on the details of Jessica's situation with Michael.

"So have I got this straight?" Todd asked in a whisper. "You're going to meet Michael after school and pretend you're Elizabeth?"

"Exactly!" said Elizabeth.

"But you *are* Elizabeth," Todd said, looking confused.

"Yes, but Michael thinks *Jessica* is Elizabeth," she explained.

"So you're going to pretend you're Elizabeth, but not the Elizabeth that *Jessica* has been pretending to be," Todd said.

"Right. A very *un*clumsy Elizabeth, in fact," Elizabeth added.

"So then Michael is going to realize that he's really in love with Jessica," Todd concluded.

"Exactly," Elizabeth said.

"Liz, you're brilliant," said Todd. "I knew there was a reason I was in love with you."

"At last," said Elizabeth, "a man who loves me for my mind."

"But not only your mind," Todd said, drawing her close to him and nibbling on her ears. "Also your ears."

"Todd!" Elizabeth exclaimed in mock astonishment, pushing him gently away from her. "Here? In front of all your fans?"

"I don't think they'll mind," said Todd with a grin. His statement was greeted with a chorus of catcalls from the guys at the table.

"We don't mind!" A.J. Morgan yelled out. "We like it!"

"More, more!" hooted Jason Mann.

"Listen, I've got to run," said Elizabeth, smiling at the boys' behavior. "I'll talk to you later, OK?" Now there was one more stop she needed to make.

"Oh, hi, Michael," she said, walking casually by his table. She put on one of Jessica's flashy smiles. He was sitting alone at a corner table, his head buried in a book.

"Elizabeth!" Michael said, surprised. "How are you?"

"Fine, thanks. Listen, I got your note," Elizabeth said brusquely. "Catch you at three, OK?"

She was gone before he could say a word.

Michael sat in his car after school, waiting nervously for Elizabeth to appear. He bit his lip anxiously, wondering if the tall, brown-haired guy he'd seen her with was her boyfriend. He figured he must be—they sure acted like it. But he couldn't help seeing if he had a chance with her—no matter how small. *She's so beautiful and vibrant,* he thought. *How could she ever be interested in someone as awkward and shy as I am?*

But then he reminded himself of her clumsiness. *She's a human being, just like you are,* Michael reassured himself. He remembered how he had caught her with her hand stuck in the mailbox, how she had locked herself in her locker, how her skirt had flown up in the parking lot. He smiled. She was so endearing. He felt as though he knew her already.

Just then Elizabeth showed up, chewing gum and sporting Ray Bans. She opened the door before he could reach over and hopped in the car.

"Hey, Michael, how's it goin'?" she asked coolly. "I'm on Calico Drive."

"Hi, Elizabeth." Michael smiled at her hesitatingly.

Elizabeth raised her face to the sun through the sunroof and closed her eyes. "Long day, huh? Man, school can be such a hassle."

Michael stared at her in bewilderment. Where was the unassuming, clumsy girl he was expecting, the girl full of life and energy? Who was this cool, collected bore sitting next to him?

"Thanks for the flowers," Elizabeth said distantly. "Nice gesture. I was a little surprised at first, but then

126

I realized you were just being sarcastic with the clumsiness stuff. Playing on the twin thing, I guess."

"Uh, you're welcome," said Michael, thoroughly confused.

"So, how's it goin' in Sweet Valley?" asked Elizabeth, making inane small talk. "Enjoying the California sunshine?"

"Uh, yeah, nice weather," said Michael.

"Wanna listen to some tunes?" asked Elizabeth, cracking her gum.

"Oh, sure, good idea," said Michael awkwardly. He reached for the radio dial and flipped it on.

"You got any preferences?" Elizabeth inquired.

"Oh, no, whatever you like," said Michael agreeably.

"How 'bout WZZT? Great hard rock," said Elizabeth, turning the knob deftly to the station. Instantly blaring heavy-metal music filled the car. "Cool song!" she said, tapping her foot along with the jarring music. She had actually never heard the song before in her life.

"I'm glad you like it," said Michael, forcing a smile.

Elizabeth closed her eyes again and leaned back in the seat, basking in the sunshine coming in through the window and humming along to the music.

Michael drove in silence, gripping the steering wheel so tightly that his knuckles turned white.

"Well, I think this is it," he said, pulling up in front of the Wakefields' split-level house on Calico Drive. Elizabeth opened her eyes and straightened up.

"Hey," she said, "how did you recognize the house?"

127

"Oh, I remembered it from the day you were . . . you were, uh, you know, caught in the mailbox," Michael said, smiling over at her.

Elizabeth looked at him with a puzzled look on her face. "Caught in the mailbox?" She looked at him as though he were crazy, then shrugged, seeming to dismiss the thought. "Well, whatever," she said, jumping out of the car. "Thanks for the lift. See ya!"

Michael stared after her, perplexed. Suddenly it dawned on him. *Playing on the twin thing,* she had said. He had the wrong twin! It was *Jessica* he was in love with!

Just then the front door opened and Jessica bolted out, a set of car keys jangling in her hands. "I'm taking the Jeep," she yelled back into the house. "I'm going over to Bruce's house to study. Be back soon!" Jessica ran down the front stoop and stumbled on the bottom step, somersaulting neatly across the lawn.

Michael opened the door, meaning to help her, but she was already up and dusting herself off, apparently unhurt. Shaking her head ruefully, Jessica skipped down the lawn to the sidewalk, but stopped suddenly at the sight of Michael's car. He smiled and waved at her, gunning the engine. Jessica waved back and turned toward the house. "Bye, Jessica!" she shouted at the top of her lungs. Then she ran quickly to the Jeep, got in, and roared off.

Aha, Michael thought, *caught in the act!* He smiled to himself as he drove down peaceful Calico Drive. So Jessica had been posing as Elizabeth to hide her embarrassment. And playing it cool to cover her awkwardness. Now Michael was even more intrigued than before. Jessica was quirkier than he had thought. Suddenly it hit him—Jessica was just like him. After all, hadn't he spent his life hiding his shyness by pretending to be cool—walking slowly, saying little, keeping to himself? Obviously Jessica was doing the same thing. Had he found his soul mate?

Chapter 11

Bruce watched as Jessica picked a huge tortilla chip from the wooden bowl, covered it lavishly with salsa, and dropped it whole into her mouth. "Mmm, good," she said, crunching loudly.

"How ladylike," said Bruce sarcastically, thinking of Pamela and her perfect good manners.

Jessica batted her eyelashes at him and grabbed a few more chips. Bruce and Jessica were sitting on the plush carpet of the Patmans' luxurious living room.

Earlier that day, Jessica had cornered Bruce in the hall between classes. "Plan Three, coming up," she had said, and he'd agreed to meet her at his place after school.

"Where's Elizabeth?" Bruce asked, eager for the buffering effect of his preferred twin.

"Oh, she can't make it today. The poor thing's got a backlog of chores to do," Jessica said with a self-satisfied smile.

"Terrific," said Bruce. "I guess that makes just the

131

two of us." He picked up the wooden bowl and headed for the kitchen to get more tortilla chips, wondering how much more of Jessica Wakefield he was going to be able to take.

When Bruce had returned, she was settled on the floor, her knees drawn up and her back leaning against the Patmans' leather couch. "Now, what are your mother's favorite flowers?" Jessica asked. She had been disappointed when Elizabeth's flowers hadn't been for her, but they'd given her an idea.

"How should I know?" Bruce answered.

"Oh, come on, you must have an idea," Jessica prodded. "I mean, you may not be brilliant, but you aren't entirely dense."

Bruce threw her a hostile look.

"What *color* flower does she like?" asked Jessica, taking another tack.

"As if I would know what color flowers my mother likes!" Bruce exploded.

"Temper, temper," Jessica said, making light of his temperamental nature. "Down, boy!"

"Grrr," Bruce growled at her, pulling back his lips and baring his teeth. He grinned in spite of himself.

"Well," said Jessica, "would you by chance know what *color* your mother likes? I mean, I know you've only been living with her for sixteen years. . . ."

"Not anymore," Bruce said, his face clouding over. He shook his head quickly and turned his attention back to the problem at hand. "Her favorite color," he said thoughtfully, glancing around the tastefully decorated living room. His mother had spent weeks working with a private designer to furnish the room. It was done primarily in shades of black and gold. The antique gold lamps and embroidered Chinese rugs woven with strands of gold added a subtle, rich hue to the black leather sofas and black lacquer coffee table. "She seems to like gold," he said finally.

"Gold?" asked Jessica. "Gold flowers?"

"Well, yellow, then," said Bruce.

"Gold-yellow flowers," Jessica mused, considering. "Goldenrod!" she exclaimed suddenly.

"What's goldenrod?" asked Bruce.

"They're flowers, you idiot. Yellow flowers," Jessica said, exasperated. "We're going to have strong, sensitive Hank send mushy Marie some goldenrod," she explained. "Cancers are romantic and determined, Aries are emotional. So if your father makes a *romantic* gesture and sends your *emotional* mother flowers . . ."

Bruce looked at her skeptically. "You think she'd buy it?"

"Aries are totally impulsive," Jessica said with certainty. "They love spontaneity."

"You think some dumb flowers are going to sway my mother?" Bruce asked, unconvinced.

"Not *some*, Bruce—lots. Lots and lots of flowers. We'll fill her house with flowers," Jessica said, waving her arms around enthusiastically.

"Now, that sounds more like my father," said Bruce. "When he does something, he does it to the hilt. He always goes all-out."

Jessica had already jumped up and was punching numbers on the sleek black phone. "Yes, hello," she was saying. "We're interested in ordering some flowers. Do you carry goldenrod?

133

"They've got it!" Jessica whispered to Bruce, handing him the phone.

"Uh, hello?" said Bruce. "Yes, that's right. Goldenrod . . . My name? Henry Patman . . . Yes, please include a card. . . . How many do we want? Well, how many have you got? . . . Uh, we'll take them all."

Elizabeth ran the vacuum cleaner across the living-room rug, wiping a dirty hand across her moist forehead. She felt as though she had been cleaning for days. She had dusted and vacuumed the entire house, scrubbed the bathrooms until the fixtures shined, and mopped and waxed the Spanish-tiled kitchen floor. Now it was Friday, and she was beat.

"Liz!" her mother called from the kitchen. "Could you get that?" Elizabeth turned off the vacuum cleaner and heard the sound of the phone ringing.

"Hello?" she asked, picking up the receiver.

"Oh, hi, Liz! It's Lila. Is Jessica there?" Lila sounded as though she was in high spirits.

"No, sorry, she's not home yet. Do you want—" Elizabeth hesitated as she heard the sound of the front door opening. "Oh, wait a minute, I think she's here," she said.

"Jess!" Elizabeth yelled as her sister walked in the front door. "Phone's for you!"

Jessica ran into the living room. "Thanks, Cinderella," she said, taking the phone from her sister.

Elizabeth looked down and took in her attire. She was wearing baggy old cotton sweats and an oversize man's white cotton shirt. Her hair was pulled back from her forehead with a blue bandanna, and a bucket full of cleaning goods stood by her feet. "Humph," she said, turning the vacuum cleaner back on and continuing to vacuum the carpet.

"On second thought, I'll take it in the kitchen," Jessica said, running out of the living room.

A few minutes later, Jessica slammed down the phone. Lila had only called to gloat about her upcoming date. She had given her every last detail of the impending evening. Lila had even outlined each item of her beach outfit, from her designer sandals to her matching straw beach bag.

Jessica took a deep breath and quickly composed herself. She had an idea. Turning to her mother, who was sitting at the butcher-block table doing paperwork, she said, "Hey, Mom, can I help with dinner?" She gave her mother a sugarcoated smile.

Mrs. Wakefield turned to look at her daughter.

"Why are looking at me like that?" Jessica asked.

"What have you done with the real Jessica?" Mrs. Wakefield asked with a sparkle in her eye.

"Oh, come on. I help sometimes! You're not giving me enough credit." Was the whole world turning against her?

"Maybe you're right. I'm sorry, dear. Of course you can help. But you know it's your sister's job this week."

"I know. I just thought I'd help her out. Sisterly love and all that." Jessica sat down on a stool and picked up a red onion from the pile of vegetables on the kitchen counter.

"Liz!" Mrs. Wakefield called. "Time to start dinner!"

Jessica bent her head and started chopping the

135

onion. She let out a long, dramatic sigh and looked up to see how her mother was reacting. She hadn't seemed to notice.

"OK, I'm ready, Mom," Elizabeth said, appearing on the threshold of the kitchen, looking tired and bedraggled. "Chicken, right?" she asked, wiping her forehead and rolling up her sleeves. Mrs. Wakefield nodded, and Elizabeth headed to the refrigerator.

"Hey, Liz, I suppose you heard about the beach barbecue tonight, the one the entire junior class is having?" Jessica asked casually.

"Yeah, I heard," said Elizabeth with a sigh as she stood at the kitchen sink, washing the chicken. Enid had come running up to her at school with the news. Elizabeth was disappointed that she would miss the party. She had barely seen her friends or her boyfriend the entire week.

"I guess we can't go, because we're still grounded," Jessica said in a resigned tone. "Right, Mom?" she added, looking at her mother hopefully.

"I guess not," Mrs. Wakefield agreed calmly.

"Mom, could we please, please just go to this one party?" Jessica pleaded. "It's *extremely* important."

"Jessica, what would be the point of being grounded if you could go out when you wanted to?" Mrs. Wakefield asked.

"I promise I won't ever ask for anything else. And you could ground us for an extra day. That's it! We'll stay grounded until Monday night!" Jessica exclaimed, looking extremely pleased with her idea. "What do you think, Liz?"

Elizabeth looked at her mother hopefully.

"Girls, the answer is no. And there will be no fur-

136

ther discussion about it," Mrs. Wakefield said firmly.

"I'll never get to Michael now," Jessica wailed, still chopping the onion. "By sunset tonight Lila will have her claws firmly implanted in him."

Elizabeth looked at her sister and wondered if the tears on her cheeks were from Lila beating her out or from the onion.

Michael and Lila walked across the sand to the beach party by the water. It was another hot, sultry night and sounds of music and laughter greeted their ears as they approached the lively beach barbecue.

Michael stood at the top of a sand dune, gazing down at the sight before him. A grill had been set up in the sand, and the smell of barbecued hamburgers and hot dogs wafted up to him. A group of kids wearing shorts and bathing suits were playing volleyball across a net in the sand. Other kids were throwing Frisbees and footballs. Couples were scattered across the sand, talking and cuddling together.

What in the world am I doing here? Michael thought as he took in the happy scene. He wanted to run into the water and swim to the other side of the ocean. When Lila had invited him to the party, his first instinct had been to say no. Even though she was a popular, pretty girl, with her long wavy hair and deep brown eyes, rich society girls weren't his type. But, he had told himself, he had vowed to be more sociable. So he had accepted the invitation, thinking he might find Elizabeth Wakefield here. When he had found out that it was Jessica he really wanted, he had been even more determined to come. After all, she did seem to spend all her time with Lila.

Lila stared contentedly at the scene in front of her. It was a magical night. It seemed as though everybody from the junior class was there. *Except my competition*, Lila thought smugly.

"Boy-gers, get your boy-gers," Winston yelled like a street vendor. He was standing by the grill with his arm around Maria Santelli.

"C'mon, Michael," Lila said, taking his arm and leading him to the group. "I'll introduce you around." She couldn't wait to show off her new prize.

Lila and Michael headed to the grill, picking up paper plates and loading them with burgers and chips. "Hey, let's go over there," Lila said, spotting Amy sitting with a group of kids on a large blanket spread out on the sand.

Michael, awkwardly balancing his plate, followed her.

"Hi, everybody," Lila said, smiling like a cat basking in the sun. "This is Michael." She introduced Michael to everybody there. Amy Sutton was curled up with her tennis-star boyfriend, Barry Rork. Caroline Pearce and Pamela Robertson were sitting cross-legged in the sand nearby, plates of food in front of them. Jeannie West and Sandra Bacon were huddled together on their own blanket, engrossed in conversation.

Michael greeted everybody, feeling like an outsider among such good friends. Lila sat down on the blanket, drawing her knees up and taking a bite out of her burger. She gave him an encouraging smile. Michael gave her a tentative smile back, and sat down awkwardly.

"Well, what's the verdict?" asked Winston, strolling

over in his goofy white chef's hat and apron. "How's the grub?"

His question met with a chorus of approval. "Mmmm," said Amy.

"Yummy," added Caroline.

Lila gave him a thumbs-up sign.

"Phew, thank the stars! I feel dizzy with relief," Winston joked. He wandered back to help Ken with the cooking.

Lila and her friends made small talk, eating enthusiastically. From time to time she smiled at Michael, noticing that he wasn't joining in the conversation. Still, she thought, he didn't seem unhappy. Maybe he was just shy, although that was pretty unbelievable with a guy as gorgeous as he was.

After they had eaten and thrown their paper plates and utensils into the beach's trash cans, people started pairing up on their blankets. Lila stayed and talked quietly with Amy and Barry, sometimes punctuating her statements with a gentle pat on Michael's arm.

Soon it was dark on the beach, and someone made a small fire. Winston came over with Maria, falling to his knees onto the blanket and pulling her down with him.

"Winston!" Maria laughed, tumbling down onto him.

Lila lay back on the blanket and looked up at the sky. It was so beautiful and peaceful, and best of all, she knew Jessica was at home, eating her heart out. "Hey, look, a shooting star!" she said, pointing to the sky. "It's a sign."

Winston looked up at the sky. "That's not a shooting star, Lila. It's Mercury. And it's on its way to the earth! Aaak!" he yelled, falling facedown on the blanket and shielding his body with his arms. "Hit the deck! It's a crashing planet!"

Everyone laughed except for Lila, who was not amused. "Hey, Winston, see that constellation over there?" she said, pointing up to the sky. "That's *your* symbol. The Big Dipper."

Winston laughed good-naturedly.

Michael sat uncomfortably on the blanket with Lila, watching the merriment before him. He casually twirled a stick around in the sand, considering the possibility of burying himself up to the neck.

Lila looked over at Michael's handsome profile. "So, Michael," Lila said, "are you having a good time?"

"Yeah, great," he mumbled.

"Hey," said Caroline. "Where do you think the Wakefields are?"

"I think they're at home sulking," Lila said cheerfully. "They're grounded for the week."

"Well," said Caroline, her green eyes bright, "I don't believe it. I think that's just an excuse." She lowered her voice, drawing everybody's attention to her. "It just so happens that I've seen a certain Wakefield twin and a certain snobby senior together after school numerous times this week."

"Yeah, that's right. We saw Bruce and Elizabeth at the Dairi Burger on Tuesday," said Amy.

"They were acting kind of funny, weren't they?" added Barry.

Just then Bruce sauntered down the beach and approached their blanket.

"Well, speak of the devil!" said Ken.

"Hey, Patman, what are you doing, crashing our party?" joked Winston. "You're too old for this."

"Well, I didn't want your little gathering to be a total failure," said Bruce, taking a seat on the blanket near Pamela. He looked at her and smiled, making it clear why he was there. Pamela mustered a weak smile and turned back to the group.

Bruce sighed and looked around him, noticing Michael sitting next to Lila. "Hey, Hampton," he said. "You're a gate-crasher too, huh?"

"Yeah, guess so," Michael responded.

"No, Bruce, Michael was *invited*," Lila said haughtily.

Bruce ignored Lila, his longtime archenemy, and turned to Michael again. "There's something I want to talk to you about," he said, bringing his head close to Michael's. Bruce gave him a hard sell on the merits of Phi Epsilon, providing a complete rundown of the workings of the fraternity. "So, hazing starts next week if you're interested, man," Bruce finished.

"Thanks," said Michael. "I'll think about it and let you know."

"Hey, Bruce, where's Liz?" asked Caroline.

Bruce sent her a withering look, glancing over at Pamela anxiously. She was looking down at the blanket.

"How should I know?" he snapped.

"Yeah, Bruce," Barry chimed in. "We want to know why you've been spending so much time with Elizabeth."

"Inquiring minds want to know," Amy said, giggling.

Bruce fell silent, unsure as to how to respond. Were they baiting him, aware that Elizabeth had dumped him to go back to that stuffy Wilkins? "Don't you *juniors* have more interesting things to talk about?" he asked gruffly. Suddenly Pamela stood up quietly with her bag and slipped away unnoticed from the group. Bruce watched her leave in dismay. When she'd gotten a few yards away, she broke into a run. Bruce watched helplessly as she ran down the beach, following her course with his eyes until she became a little speck on the horizon.

Michael also watched Pamela disappear, yearning to run down the beach as she had. He didn't know how much more of this party he could take. Lila and Bruce together were just too much for him in one night. "Uh, Lila," he said finally, turning to her. "I think I'm about ready to go. What about you?"

"What?" She stared at him openmouthed. "But the party has only gotten started. There are going to be games and dancing and probably a huge bonfire."

The prospect of enduring hours more of the party was more than Michael could stomach. "I'm really sorry," he said. "Can I give you a ride home?"

"I can get a ride with someone else, thanks," Lila said, flipping her hair off her shoulders. Her face flushed with anger as Michael said good-bye to the group and walked off. How dare he humiliate her this way! She got up and stood in the sand, clenching her fists. What a jerk!

"Hundreds and hundreds of flowers!" Jessica said excitedly, updating Elizabeth on the latest plan on Saturday morning. Jessica had spent the entire evening sulking in her room, refusing to speak to anyone, including her sister. But she had just gotten the scoop about Lila's failure at the beach party from Amy on the phone, and her spirits had lifted considerably. "So what do you think?"

"Jessica, it's perfect," Elizabeth agreed, grabbing a ripe cantaloupe from the refrigerator. "The whole house covered with yellow flowers—beautiful, cheerful yellow flowers. And the scent! Can you imagine?"

"Yep! It's quite a plan, if I do say so myself," said Jessica with a self-satisfied smile. She took a banana from the ceramic fruit bowl in the middle of the kitchen table and sliced it into her carton of strawberry yogurt. Elizabeth sat down with Jessica at the butcher-block table and began carving the melon into fourths.

Hmm, Elizabeth thought, breathing in the fragrant air of the hot California morning. *Maybe things are beginning to look up.* Suddenly the calm of the morning was broken as a car screeched into the driveway. Elizabeth ran to the living-room window to find Bruce striding up to the house with a fierce expression on his face.

"Jessica!" Elizabeth warned. "It's Bruce, and he looks like he's ready to kill someone."

"Tell him I'm out with Lila," Jessica yelped, making her way up the stairs two at a time.

Bruce leaned heavily against the doorbell.

"Where is she?" he growled furiously as Elizabeth opened the door.

"Who?" asked Elizabeth innocently.

"That conniving twin sister of yours who's trying to ruin any chances my parents have of getting back together," said Bruce.

"Um, she's out with Lila. Why don't you just sit

down," Elizabeth said soothingly, leading Bruce to the kitchen and pulling out a chair. "I'll fix you some lemonade."

"Goldenrod, she says—goldenrod," Bruce ranted. "Goldenrod!"

"What happened, Bruce?" Elizabeth looked at him inquiringly.

"Guess what flower my mother is allergic to, Liz. *Highly* allergic to," Bruce demanded.

"Goldenrod?" Elizabeth said quietly.

"You guessed it." Bruce laughed maniacally. "And guess where my mother is now? No, I'll tell you. My mother is in the hospital, due to a severe allergic reaction to goldenrod, a severe allergic reaction that almost *killed* her!" he yelled.

"Oh no," said Elizabeth, clapping her hand to her mouth.

"Oh yes," said Bruce. "So now I think, giving all things their due, it's Jessica's turn to be killed."

"Bruce," said Elizabeth, adopting her most reasonable tone, "Jessica couldn't have known your mother was allergic to goldenrod. If anything, *you* should have known it."

"*I* should have known it!" Bruce yelled, his eyes flashing. "How could I have known that my mother was allergic to some bizarre strain of yellow flowers?"

"All I'm trying to say," Elizabeth said, "is that you shouldn't take out your own frustration on Jessica. She had the very best intentions. And you know it."

"I know only one thing," Bruce said, standing up. "My mother has been suffering tremendously, living alone in a house across town, my parents are further apart than ever—and now," his voice broke, "my

144

mother is in the hospital. So just give your dear little sister this message—" Bruce spit out the words. "I don't want any more of her *help*!"

Bruce stormed out of the house and slammed the door to his Porsche shut, the wheels screeching as he tore down the street.

"Jess!" Elizabeth called, dashing up the stairs to find her sister. Jessica was sitting dejectedly on the top step, her elbows resting on her knees and her chin cupped in her hands. Elizabeth practically ran her over in her haste.

"Jessica!" she said breathlessly, plopping down next to her. "You won't believe—"

"I heard," said Jessica, who had listened to the whole conversation from the staircase. "Not so perfect, huh?"

"Not so perfect," Elizabeth agreed, shaking her head in disbelief. "Mrs. Patman's in the hospital. She's in the hospital!"

"Liz, do you mind?" Jessica asked. "I heard already. Now what are we going to do?"

"Jessica," Elizabeth cautioned, "I'm warning you, for my sake and yours, you had better come up with a good plan . . . and fast."

Chapter 12

"How's my favorite patient?" asked Mr. Patman cheerfully, his arms laden with gifts as he entered Mrs. Patman's brightly lit hospital room. He crossed the room swiftly to sit by his wife's bedside.

"Just peachy," said Mrs. Patman dryly. She looked pale and wan, lying against the crisp white sheets of the twin bed in her blue hospital gown. She had an I.V. in her left arm and a tube running to an electrocardiograph machine that was monitoring her heart.

Mr. Patman looked at his wife tenderly, brushing her hair carefully off her forehead. Her brush with death had shaken him profoundly. He had been terrified when he had received her call. "Hank! I'm having— some sort of—allergy attack. From the flowers—you sent me. I can't—breathe," she had said, gasping as she tried to get out the words. *Flowers?* he had thought in confusion. "I'll be there with an ambulance in two minutes, Marie," he had said reassuringly. "Don't panic, sweetheart." He was touched and a little surprised that she had reached out to him in an emergency.

"Feel strong enough to eat now?" Mr. Patman asked, setting a tray gently on his wife's lap. He lifted the cover of a steaming silver platter, revealing an appetizing assortment of tender chicken cutlets, steamed vegetables, and warm, freshly baked bread. Mr. Patman had refused to allow his wife to eat the meals the hospital provided. "No wife of mine is going to eat hospital food," he had said categorically. He insisted on bringing her home-cooked meals instead.

"Yes, thank you. I believe I can eat now," Mrs. Patman told her husband in a formal tone. Still nauseated from the drugs she had been given the night before, she had refused the breakfast he had brought earlier. Now she reached for the fork, but Mr. Patman lightly pushed her hand down.

"Now, now. You need to conserve your energy," he admonished gently. "Open up," he said, spearing some food with the fork and aiming it toward his wife's mouth.

"I am not an invalid!" she said, taking the fork back from him and beginning to eat. She was irritated by all his tender care. It was so hypocritical. Why wouldn't he just leave her in peace? She had told the nurse she was refusing all visitors, but her husband had insisted on seeing her.

"You know, you scared the daylights out of me," Mr. Patman said.

I'm sure, thought Mrs. Patman bitterly. *If something happened to me, there wouldn't be anybody to host your cocktail parties. To cook you dinner. To take care of your son.*

Mr. Patman looked down at his wife, wondering if he was getting through to her. She hadn't been very talkative since she'd been in the hospital. "Goldenrod—who would have ever thought?" he said. "You've never been allergic to anything. Maybe it's something you've developed."

"Maybe," said Mrs. Patman curtly.

"I don't know if I should kill Bruce or thank him," said Mr. Patman suddenly. He had called the florist the night before, and they had informed him that the flowers had indeed been charged to his account. Only one other person had access to his charge card—Bruce.

Mrs. Patman lay quietly, her heart going out to her son. She was worried about Bruce. She knew what a strain their marriage problems must be putting on him. He must be having a really hard time to have made such an effort to get them back together, she thought. She had felt terribly guilty for moving out of the house, as though she was abandoning her son. Now that the divorce proceedings had been reestablished, she felt even worse.

Mr. Patman coughed. "Well, I brought you a little reading material," he said, making another effort to reach her. He cleared away the tray and poured out the contents of a bulky shopping bag, a large assortment of books and magazines spilling onto the bed.

A little! Mrs. Patman thought, looking down at the array on her lap. He had brought enough reading material for an entire beauty salon. "I really don't know why you're going to such lengths," she said in an annoyed voice. "I'm only going to be here for the rest of the day."

"Well, I didn't know what you'd be in the mood

149

for," said Mr. Patman, smiling lightly. "Tell you what—you make your choice, and I'll read to you."

"Hank, I really think you've done enough for one day," said Mrs. Patman, anxious for him to leave. He had been at her side during her every waking moment, leaving only to buy gifts and pick up food. The sight of her unfaithful husband was making her more ill than the allergy attack had. "Don't you think you should get back to work?"

"What work?" he asked, grinning slightly.

"The Rothman-Steel building deal, for example," she said. "Isn't there a board meeting today in Washington?" In spite of herself, Marie still had all the details of his business life in her head.

"There'll be other deals," said Mr. Patman, waving his hand dismissively.

"Other deals!" said Mrs. Patman, shocked. "But this is a hundred-thousand-dollar transaction."

"Sweetheart," said Mr. Patman, taking her hand. She flinched at his touch and yanked her hand away. Mr. Patman took a deep breath and went on. "Marie, you're more important to me than anything else in the world. There is nowhere I would rather be right now than right here, by your side."

"You know what? I've had enough of your *loving* care and attention," said Mrs. Patman, her voice dripping with sarcasm. "I'd like you to leave now."

Mr. Patman stared at his wife in frustration. He didn't know how to break through to her. It seemed that all his efforts to show her how much he cared about her were useless. "Marie," he said finally, speaking in a halting voice, "about that scarf."

"I do not want to discuss Alice Wakefield's scarf,"

she snapped, turning her head away from him.

Mr. Patman looked at her imploringly. "Marie, I swear, I didn't know anything about it. I don't know how that scarf got in my pocket."

"Hank, if you don't leave right now, I'm going to ring for the nurse," warned Mrs. Patman. She had had enough of her husband's lies and excuses. She held her hand threateningly above the call button by the side of the bed, poised to press it at any moment. "And I want to reschedule our meeting with the Traceys as soon as possible," she added. "To sign the divorce papers."

Mr. Patman stood to go. "Fine!" he said angrily. He had made a valiant effort. If this was the way she wanted it, it was fine by him. If his wife wanted a divorce, she would get it. Mr. Patman turned and walked out the door, letting it close shut behind him.

Mrs. Patman lay back and turned her head, tears trickling slowly out of the corners of her eyes. Why was he playing with her emotions this way? Why wouldn't he just admit the truth and allow her to get on with her life? But she knew why: He wanted to have his affair and his wife as well. *Well*, she thought stubbornly, *he can't have his cake and eat it too.*

"So, I hear Michael left the beach barbecue early," said Jessica, trying not to gloat. Jessica and Lila were stretched out on matching chaise longues by the side of the sparkling Wakefield pool, soaking in the hot rays of the Saturday-afternoon sun.

Lila snorted. "What a bore! Looks like he's going to be hanging out with Bruce. Bruce was laying it on thick about Phi Ep."

"Really?" said Jessica, her ears perking up.

"Yeah, you can have him," Lila said in disgust.

"Gee, thanks, Li," said Jessica, smiling quietly to herself. At least Lila was out of the picture. Now she just had to get him to pay more attention to her.

Lila waved her hand magnanimously. "No problem," she said, turning a fraction of an inch to work on her tan. Keeping her body perfectly still, she reached over to the deck to flip through the stations of the portable radio.

"Lila, if you keep turning yourself like that, you're going to roast like an animal," Jessica said, sitting up to smooth suntan lotion on her legs.

"I'm telling you, Jessica, timing is *everything*," Lila insisted, barely moving her lips as she spoke. "Fifteen minutes on each side. One hour later, you've got a beautiful, even tan."

"Fifteen minutes on each side?" Jessica repeated. "How many sides have you got?" She took a long swallow from her ice-cold lemonade, dabbing her moist forehead with the cool glass.

"Four, of course," Lila explained. "Two-sided tanning is a fallacy. You can't just do front and back—you have to do both sides, too."

"Really?" asked Jessica. "OK, which side are you on now?"

"Right side up, right cheek to the sun, chin back," Lila ordered.

Jessica assumed the posture Lila was describing. "How long do we have to hold this?" she complained, wriggling around impatiently.

"Fifteen minutes, obviously," explained Lila, "and then we do the left side."

Jessica lay back and closed her eyes. "Well," she said in a tantalizingly slow voice. "I've got some gossip to help us pass the time."

Lila turned to face her eagerly.

"Lila! We're doing the right side," Jessica scolded.

"OK, let's have it," Lila demanded, turning her face back to the left.

"Only if you swear you won't tell anyone," Jessica said, lowering her voice to a whisper. "This is *strictly* confidential."

"What could be so strictly confidential?" Lila asked.

"Bruce's parents, that's what," Jessica said triumphantly.

"Oh, really, Jessica," Lila scoffed. "You actually think I would waste my time spreading around boring gossip about Bruce's parents?"

"Oh, so you're not interested?" Jessica asked.

"Well, I didn't say I wasn't interested. . . ." Lila responded.

Just then the sliding glass door to the patio opened, and Elizabeth came out. "What are you two doing in that ridiculous position?" she exclaimed upon finding Jessica and Lila stretched out dramatically on the chaise longues, their faces turned sharply to the left and their heads flung back.

"We're attaining the perfect California tan," explained Jessica.

"Oh, I see," Elizabeth said. "Hi, Lila."

"Hi, Elizabeth," Lila said, checking her watch and turning over on her right side.

"Left side now, Jessica," Lila ordered.

Elizabeth shook her head, not surprised to see

Lila so concerned with such trivial matters. "Uh, Lila, do you think you could excuse us for a minute?" Elizabeth asked.

"Sure," said Lila, not moving her head as she spoke.

"C'mon, Jess," Elizabeth said urgently, yanking her sister up by the arm. "We've got important business to discuss."

"All right, all right, I'm coming," Jessica grumbled, grabbing her lemonade and following Elizabeth across the white pavement to a couple of lawn chairs clustered together in the far corner of the pool area.

"Jessica, how could you be lounging by the pool at a time like this?" Elizabeth demanded.

"Liz, I was *thinking*!" Jessica said. "The sun relaxes me. It's good for the central nervous system."

"OK, then," Elizabeth said, pulling her chair close to her sister. "Let's have it."

"We-ll," said Jessica slowly, stalling for time, "I think there's only one possible solution at this point."

Elizabeth looked at her expectantly.

"I think it's time, it's time . . ." Jessica said haltingly, looking around the patio. She could hear the soft sounds of Jamie Peters's latest single playing on the radio. The radio suddenly gave her an idea.

"I think it's time to get Mom involved," Jessica said decisively.

"Jess, she'll never agree. You know how Mom feels about privacy," Elizabeth protested.

"Who's asking her to agree?" asked Jessica with a wicked grin on her face. She lowered her voice to a whisper. "You corner Mom and get her to reveal *everything* about why it never worked with Hank Patman and why it never would. You can hide my mini-recorder in your jacket. It'll be positive proof that they're not having an affair."

"But why would I be asking?" Elizabeth asked.

"Tell her it's for a continuation of your English biography project," Jessica suggested. Elizabeth had spent her spring break working on a biography of her mother for her English class. After all she had discovered about her mother the week before, her paper had turned out to be closer to a soap opera than a biographical sketch. Mr. Collins, who was not only Elizabeth's favorite English teacher and the *Oracle* adviser, but also a good friend, had been impressed with the outcome.

"I don't know, Jess." Elizabeth hesitated, uncomfortable with the idea of scheming on her mother.

"C'mon, Liz, you're the reporter in the family. You're the only person in the world who can do this!" Jessica begged. "And besides, it's for a good cause. Mom would understand."

"Oh, all right, I guess," Elizabeth agreed, thinking that their mother hadn't been quite up front with them in the past. "But I can't do it until later this afternoon. Todd and I are going for a walk along the beach."

"You're going for a walk at a time like this?" Jessica said jokingly, throwing Elizabeth's words back at her.

"It'll be about the first time I've spent any time alone with Todd this whole week," said Elizabeth.

"But, Liz, we're still grounded," Jessica reminded her.

155

"I know. But Mom said I could take this one walk," Elizabeth explained. "I think she feels sorry for me because I've been slaving away, cooking dinners and cleaning the house all week."

"That figures," Jessica said. Elizabeth always got off easy.

"But you know, Jess," said Elizabeth, thinking. "We really should do a test case first—just to make sure we can hide the mini-recorder properly and hear the words clearly."

"Yeah, an experimental tape," Jessica agreed. "Lila and I will do it, since you have plans."

"Great," Elizabeth said. Then her face fell. "No, we promised Bruce we wouldn't tell anyone else about it."

Jessica looked away quickly, but not before Elizabeth read her guilty expression.

"Jessica! You told Lila!" Elizabeth said accusingly.

"I'm sorry, Liz. It was an accident! She *is* my best friend. And she promised not to tell anyone."

"I can't believe it," Elizabeth said, shaking her head. "Come Monday, the whole school's going to be talking about this."

"To tell you the truth, Liz, I don't think she found the story too interesting. And besides," said Jessica, looking at her sister suspiciously, "didn't you tell Todd?"

Suddenly they heard a horn beep from the driveway.

"Oh, there he is!" Elizabeth said. "See you later, Jess!" She gave her sister a quick wave and ran through the screen door into the house.

Jessica stared after her sister, smiling. Sometimes she and Elizabeth were more alike than people thought!

Jessica and Lila sat comfortably under umbrellas on the patio, deciding it was time to shade themselves from the hot rays of the sweltering afternoon sun. Jessica hid her mini-recorder under her white terry-cloth wrap and pressed the record button. "Testing," she said. "Testing, one, two, three."

"Jessica, I bet Elizabeth isn't really out with Todd at all," Lila said suddenly. "I bet she's with Bruce, carrying on a secret love affair. Maybe they're at the beach right now, having a little afternoon rendezvous."

"No way," Jessica said with certainty. "Bruce isn't her type."

"Well, they did make out in front of the entire school last weekend," Lila persisted. "Maybe Elizabeth wants a little more spice in her life."

"Maybe," mused Jessica, considering the possibility. "After all, Todd Wilkins *is* the most boring guy in the entire universe."

"Not that Liz is exactly the life of the party," Lila put in.

"Well, who knows what lurks underneath that calm exterior," Jessica said.

"The heart of a wild woman," Lila speculated jokingly.

"Nah," Jessica said finally, waving a dismissive hand. "Bruce Patman is the last person my sister would be interested in. And all Bruce cares about are his parents. And his Porsche."

"So, it looks like the Patmans' marriage is falling apart," Lila said with glee. Nothing gave her more pleasure than witnessing the collapse of the Patman household, her family's greatest rivals.

"Not if I can help it," Jessica said, adjusting her sunglasses on her nose.

"Jessica, I'm telling you, this tape thing is never going to work," Lila scoffed.

"The tape!" Jessica said. She looked down at the tape rolling slowly in the recorder. "We've been taping ourselves the whole time! Well, I guess we've got our test case," she said, rewinding the tape to hear the results.

Chapter 13

Elizabeth pulled off her leather sandals and wiggled her toes, enjoying the feel of the hot white sand under her bare feet. She gathered her sandals together in her left hand and reached for Todd's hand with the other.

"Perfect day for a picnic," Todd remarked as they walked along the shore together, shifting his picnic basket to take her hand in his.

"Mmm," Elizabeth agreed, preoccupied with thoughts of the Patman situation.

Todd looked at Elizabeth's troubled face and leaned over to kiss her tenderly on the cheek. "Something on your mind?" he asked.

"Oh—" Elizabeth hesitated, not wanting to burden Todd with her troubles with Bruce. This was practically their first time together all week, and she didn't want to spoil it. "No, no," she said, smiling up at him.

"C'mon, now," Todd said, lightly chucking her under the chin.

"No, really, Todd," Elizabeth said, making an effort to look cheerful. She smiled brightly at him and said, "It's a beautiful day, isn't it?"

"Uh-oh! She's withholding information!" Todd yelled, tackling her to the ground. "False representation! And they're fighting," he said in a Howard Cosell voice. "Ladies and gentlemen, they're fighting. And she's down! One, two, three . . . ten! She's out! Ladies and gentlemen, she's out! Out for withholding information!"

Elizabeth laughing, he gently pinned her down, smothering her lips in a passionate kiss.

For a few moments they kissed deeply, lost to the world around them. Then Todd pulled back. "Really, Liz," he said, his voice turning serious. He took her chin and turned her face toward him. "What's on your mind? I'm here for you, you know."

"Oh, Todd," Elizabeth said, relieved. "It's just that everything is going wrong. I'm starting to believe all that baloney about the planets that Jessica's been spouting. Everything we've tried has ended in disaster, and I don't even know if we're doing the right thing. I think my mom was right—butting into the Patmans' lives is only destroying them. It's all our fault."

"Now, c'mon, Liz," Todd soothed her. "Your intentions were good."

"Our intentions, yes. But the *outcome* . . ." Elizabeth's eyes blurred with tears of frustration.

"Hey, hey, c'mere," Todd said softly, cradling Elizabeth's head in his arms. He caressed her cheek gently, brushing back loose strands of blond hair from her face. Elizabeth closed her eyes, feeling herself relax as she lay in Todd's arms.

"So what's going on now?" he asked when she finally pulled herself up to a sitting position.

"Well, Jessica's latest and greatest plan is to capture all of Mom's thoughts about Mr. Patman on tape," Elizabeth explained, sitting cross-legged in the sand.

"That sounds like a good idea," said Todd. "I mean, Mrs. Patman may not trust her husband, but she'll certainly believe your mom. If she hears your mom saying that she's not having an affair, well, then, there are no two ways about it."

"I guess you're right," Elizabeth said. "But Todd, what if this doesn't work? I mean, what if the tape unravels, or if Mr. Patman intercepts it, or if Mrs. Patman has some unknown medical reaction to cassettes?"

Todd smiled at Elizabeth's active imagination. "Well, then, you'll just come up with another plan," he said.

"But, Todd, we're running out of time," Elizabeth said.

"You know, Liz," Todd said thoughtfully, "I think there's only so much you can do to help people. At some point they've got to help themselves. So, if the Patmans still don't get back together after all your efforts, then maybe they weren't meant to be together. I mean, it's their life—not Bruce's, not yours."

Elizabeth sat back in Todd's arms, thinking about what he'd said. Todd was right. Just because she wanted things to work out a certain way didn't mean they should. It wasn't her right to force the Patmans' destiny.

"You're right, Todd," Elizabeth said, finally at

peace with herself. "We can only do our best, and if that doesn't work, then I guess it wasn't meant to be."

"Exactly," Todd said.

"Now, would you please tell me what's in that basket?" Elizabeth asked, eyeing the picnic basket that Todd had been carrying all morning.

"Oh, this little thing?" Todd asked, turning back the cover of the oversize wicker basket. "Just a little lunch for my grounded girl."

Later Saturday afternoon Elizabeth bounced into the kitchen with a composition book in hand. "Hi, Mom!"

Mrs. Wakefield jumped and turned from the salad she was preparing. "Liz, you scared me! What are you looking so cheerful about?" she asked, taking in her daughter's rosy cheeks.

"Oh, I don't know. Just my walk with Todd, I guess. We barely got to see each other all week because of his basketball camp and my being grounded," said Elizabeth, her eyes twinkling.

"Well, I'm glad to see you looking so happy," said Mrs. Wakefield, smiling.

"Hey, Mom?" asked Elizabeth hesitatingly.

"Yes, dear?"

"How would you like to give me an exclusive interview about you and Mr. Patman? I'm thinking of expanding my English biography project," Elizabeth explained, feeling a pang of guilt as she spoke. She could feel Jessica's mini-recorder pressing against her skirt pocket.

"Sure, honey. If you're interested," Mrs. Wakefield said agreeably.

"You would?" asked Elizabeth, relieved. "Like now?"

"No time like the present," said Mrs. Wakefield with a smile. "But do you think you could help me with the salad?"

"Of course," said Elizabeth. "We'll talk and chop."

"We'll talk chop," Mrs. Wakefield quipped.

"Mom!" Elizabeth groaned, grabbing a handful of fresh vegetables out of the refrigerator. She set them down on the kitchen table and began to sort them. Mrs. Wakefield joined her with a wooden salad bowl, a cutting board, and two sharp knives.

Half an hour later, Elizabeth flew into her sister's room, waving the tape in her hand. "Jess—I got it!"

Jessica was lying on her bed, absorbed in Linda Goodman's *Love Signs*. "You got it?" she said excitedly.

"It's perfect!" Elizabeth said. "Just what we needed."

Jessica jumped on her bed and squealed. "Let's mail it right now."

"Jess, no offense, but I think this time we should drive it over."

"No offense taken," Jessica said with a laugh. "But how are we going to find out where Mrs. Patman is living?"

"I'll get the address from Bruce. I should call him anyway and fill him in on the plan," Elizabeth said. "You prepare the package, OK?"

Soon Elizabeth and Jessica were speeding through the Sweet Valley hills in the Jeep, their spirits high as they made their way across town to Mrs.

Patman's house. They had turned the radio to their preferred radio station, WSVC, for "fifties favorites." Jessica was singing along with the music, hyped up with excitement.

"Hey, Jess, why don't we just turn off the radio?" Elizabeth teased. "I can't hear your singing over the music."

"OK, I get the point," said Jessica, switching to a low hum. She sat back in her seat, the wind whistling past them, whipping her blond hair all around her head.

"Hey, Jess," Elizabeth said.

"Hmm?"

"You've got the tape, right?"

"Here it is," Jessica said, grabbing the mini-cassette from the dashboard and holding it up proudly. "It's all here, all the evidence we could ever want, crammed into this little, mini, itty-bitty tape."

"Recorded and preserved for posterity," Elizabeth said, grinning.

"Hey, Liz," said Jessica, suddenly hit by a worrisome possibility. "What happens if Mrs. Patman is home when we get there?"

"She won't be," Elizabeth reassured her. "Bruce said she's not getting home from the hospital until late tonight."

"Well, that's good," Jessica said.

"Yeah," said Elizabeth. "At least one good thing's come from that whole flower disaster."

"So she should get the tape tonight," figured Jessica.

"If she looks in her mailbox, that is," Elizabeth said.

"How's she getting home?" Jessica asked.

"Oh, I guess Mr. Patman's going to drive her," Elizabeth speculated. "Bruce said he's been spending all his time at the hospital. Hey, I think this is her street." She craned her neck to read the street sign. "Yep, this is it. Maple Lane. It's number 202."

"Maple Lane," Jessica repeated. "Sounds like a good location for a Hitchcock murder mystery. Action, adventure, intrigue—at 202 Maple Lane."

"Geez, Jess, I never knew you were so morbid," said Elizabeth. "Do you think you could look for the number?" She drove slowly down the block while Jessica called out numbers.

"There it is, number 202," Jessica said, pointing to a small pink house on the corner.

Elizabeth coasted to a stop on the sidewalk in front of the house.

"Boy, she must have wanted to get out of Bruce's house fast," Jessica said, looking at the little house with disdain.

"Jessica, would you stop being such a snob and get to work?" Elizabeth said. "Everybody on the block can see us while we're just sitting here."

"Oh, you're right," said Jessica, grabbing the tape and running to the mailbox at the end of the drive-way. She quickly opened it and placed the tape strategically on the top of the pile of waiting letters, where Mrs. Patman would be sure to see it. Jessica closed the lid firmly and darted back to the car.

"This time you're the getaway guy," said Jessica as Elizabeth pulled away smoothly and sped down the street.

"Yeah, we're getting pretty good at this, aren't

we?" said Elizabeth, grinning at her sister.

Twenty minutes later, Elizabeth pulled into the Wakefield driveway and cut the engine. Jessica and Elizabeth hopped out of the Jeep and ran up the front walk. Elizabeth was flushed with excitement, thrilled that the drop-off had gone off without incident.

"Hey, Jess, can I borrow the mini-recorder?" Elizabeth asked on her way into the house. "I want to tape the basketball coach for my column next week. I think I'm going to try to cover the events of the Big Mesa game."

"Sure, no problem," said Jessica.

Elizabeth and Jessica walked into the foyer and shut the front door behind them. "Oh, here it is," Elizabeth said, picking up the machine off the hall table. "Can I use the sample tape?"

"Why don't I just give you a new one?" Jessica suggested, grabbing the tape recorder from her sister and quickly ejecting the tape. She handed the mini-recorder back to her sister.

Elizabeth looked at Jessica suspiciously. "Jessica, what did you put on that tape?"

"What do you mean? Nothing!" said Jessica indignantly.

"Jess—" Elizabeth said in a warning tone, putting her hand out for the tape.

"OK, OK," Jessica said, giving in and handing the tape to Elizabeth. "But don't get mad."

Elizabeth took the tape, inserted it, then rewound it to the beginning.

Jessica bit her lip as the tape began to play.

"So, Mom, what do you think attracted you to

Hank Patman in the first place?" they heard.

It's the wrong tape! thought Jessica in relief. Then her relief quickly turned to alarm.

"Well, we were young . . ." came their mother's voice.

Elizabeth abruptly shut off the tape. The two girls stared at each other in shock, the same look of horror registering in two identical pairs of blue-green eyes. Then Elizabeth's eyes hardened in anger.

Chapter 14

"Jessica, I don't know why, but I'm giving you one more chance," Bruce said. "Even though you appear to be completely incapable of performing even the simplest task."

Jessica, Elizabeth, and Bruce were at Guido's Pizza Palace Sunday afternoon, where they had met to come up with a final plan. They were sharing a large vegetarian pizza heaped with avocados, tomatoes, mushrooms, onions, and eggplant. Jessica and Elizabeth had told their parents they were going to the library to study.

"Any word from your mother about the flowers?" Elizabeth asked.

"She hasn't mentioned them to me, so I think we're safe," Bruce said. "Maybe she still thinks my father sent them as a secret gift."

"What about the tape?" Elizabeth asked nervously. Jessica and Elizabeth had decided not to tell Bruce of the previous day's fiasco, sure it would send

169

him over the edge. They hadn't quite figured out how to explain the tape that Mrs. Patman received, but they had decided to worry about that when the time came.

"No, nothing," Bruce said, looking dejected. "She just got home from the hospital last night, and I haven't seen any signs of a reconciliation."

Jessica breathed a sigh of relief, taking a second slice of pizza dripping with cheese and putting it on her plate.

"I don't even know why we're bothering," said Bruce, throwing up his hands in disgust. "I heard my dad talking to Jan Tracey this morning. They're meeting with the Traceys on Tuesday to sign the divorce papers."

Jessica and Elizabeth gasped.

"They're signing the actual divorce papers?" Jessica asked in shock. She looked down at the table.

"And your father," Elizabeth asked falteringly, "does he want the divorce?"

"No. From what I could hear, I don't think he wants to go through with it. I guess she insisted," Bruce said gloomily.

"But I thought he was spending all that time with your mother at the hospital," Elizabeth said.

"Well, I guess it didn't convince her," said Bruce.

Jessica opened her mouth to say something about Aries stubbornness, but thought better of it.

"Oh, let's just forget it. There's no hope," Bruce said, pushing back his chair abruptly and standing up. "I guess it's just not in the stars," he added bitterly, looking in Jessica's direction.

Jessica winced and looked away.

170

"Bruce Patman," Elizabeth said, standing up also. "Don't you dare walk away now," she continued, surprised by her firmness. "Stop acting like a spoiled child and sit down and make yourself useful."

Bruce hesitated, uncertain what to do. He looked at Elizabeth, at the door, and back at Elizabeth again.

"All right, all right," he grumbled finally, sitting down again. "No reason to work yourself up into a tizzy."

"So, Jessica, you said you have a plan?" Elizabeth said, taking her seat again and turning to her sister.

"Yes," said Jessica, clearing her throat. "I've come up with the plan of plans—the master plan."

Bruce and Elizabeth both looked at her, Elizabeth with a hopeful glimmer in her eyes, Bruce with a cynical expression on his face.

"Intervention," Jessica said dramatically, pausing a moment to let them absorb the word.

"Intervention?" Bruce repeated.

"We're going to intervene in your parents' destiny," Jessica explained.

"Who's going to intervene?" asked Elizabeth.

"The three of us. We're going to meet with your parents and convince them to stay together and work out their problems." Jessica sat back triumphantly, a smile on her face.

Bruce looked at her incredulously. "Isn't that a little extreme, Wakefield?"

"Drastic situations call for drastic measures," Jessica said airily.

Returning home from the "library," Jessica and Elizabeth walked in the front door of the Wakefield

171

house. The phone was ringing, and Elizabeth raced across the kitchen to pick it up.

"Hello?" she asked.

"Hi, this is Michael Hampton. Could I speak to Jessica, please?"

"Oh, hi, Michael," said Elizabeth. "You say you want to speak to Jessica?"

At last! thought Jessica. She knew that playing it cool would pay off.

"Um, I'm not sure if she's here," Elizabeth said slowly, her eyes sparkling at Jessica's.

Jessica, meanwhile, was clawing at the phone cord. "Gimme that!" she hissed at her sister.

"In fact," said Elizabeth, twisting the phone cord out of her sister's reach, "I think she might be out on a date."

Jessica lunged for the phone.

"Oh, here she is!" said Elizabeth brightly. "One moment, please."

Jessica grabbed the phone from her sister's outstretched hand, sending her a withering look. "Hello?" she said breathlessly.

"Hi, Jessica, this is Michael Hampton."

"Hi," Jessica said, her heart beating wildly.

"I was—uh—wondering if you'd like to go out sometime," Michael blurted awkwardly.

"Sure, I'd love to," Jessica said.

Michael's relief was audible. "Great, great," he said. "How about Monday night? Or maybe you're busy then," he added, suddenly insecure again.

"Yeah, actually, I *do* have plans Monday night," Jessica answered, wanting to kick herself for setting the intervention plan for Monday night. "How about

Tuesday night?" she suggested, thanking her stars that Mercury would be out of retrograde by then.

"Tuesday night would be perfect," Michael said. "About, uh, six o'clock?"

"Sure, six o'clock," Jessica agreed.

"So, I'll, uh, I'll pick you up on Tuesday night at your place," Michael said.

"Great. I'll see you then," Jessica said.

"OK. Bye, Jessica," Michael said.

"Bye, Michael," Jessica said. She put down the receiver and wheeled on her sister. "I can't believe you would do that to me! My own sister! Elizabeth Wakefield!"

"Oh, I thought *you* were Elizabeth Wakefield," Elizabeth said dryly, crossing her arms and looking straight at her sister.

A crimson flush stained Jessica's cheeks. "What do you mean?" she bluffed.

"What I mean is, you've been passing yourself off as me so you wouldn't look stupid in front of Michael Hampton," Elizabeth said. She began ticking off examples on her fingers. "The mailbox, your locker—"

Jessica interrupted her. "Now, Liz, don't get all upset. Don't you see that I had no choice? You know what the situation with Mercury has been lately. You don't think it would be fair for me to lose out on Michael just because the stars have been against me, do you? Of course you don't," she said in a rush.

Elizabeth didn't say anything. She just stood still with her arms crossed, her gaze unrelenting.

"Oh, thank you, Liz." Jessica leaned over and gave her a big hug. "I knew you'd understand. You're the best, I mean it. What did I ever do to deserve a sister like you?" She hugged Elizabeth again, her face beaming.

Elizabeth sighed heavily and rolled her eyes. She knew Jessica knew that she was a sucker for the "best sister in the world act." Always had been, always will be. "OK, fine. Fine. I guess it's OK—I don't really care what Michael thinks of me, anyway." She gave Jessica a mildly exasperated look. "But no more, you understand?"

Jessica nodded wildly. "Promise. Cross my heart and hope to die," she vowed.

"I guess your game worked, huh? You've got a date with Michael."

"I guess it did," said Jessica, smiling hugely. "Maybe I should pass myself off for you more often."

"You better not!" Elizabeth said, laughing and swatting at her sister.

"He's gone!" Bruce said to Elizabeth on the phone Sunday evening.

"Great!" said Elizabeth excitedly. "My parents have left too." The Wakefields and Mr. Patman were attending the closing dinner for the Chicago project that Alice Wakefield and Hank Patman had worked on together. It was being held at a banquet hall at a hotel in downtown Sweet Valley.

"Well, we better hurry," Bruce said. "They said the dinner will be over around eleven o'clock. We've only got a few hours before they get back."

"We'll be over in two minutes!" said Elizabeth.

Bruce hung up the phone and stared into space. On Tuesday, everything would be final. His parents would sign the divorce papers that would break apart

174

his family once and for all. Bruce fought down a feeling of panic. *This is our last chance, and it had better work,* he thought grimly.

Ten minutes later, the doorbell shook Bruce out of his reverie.

"OK, let's get cracking!" Elizabeth said excitedly when he answered the door.

"Time to take a trip down memory lane!" Jessica added.

For once, Bruce was grateful to the Wakefield twins for taking charge. He was on his last legs, ready to surrender to destiny.

"Did you talk to your parents?" Elizabeth asked as they made their way into the living room.

"Well, I caught my dad before he left. Said I wanted to talk to him alone tomorrow night. We set the meeting for seven o'clock in the screening room," Bruce explained.

"And your mom?" Elizabeth asked.

"Yeah, I called her, too. Gave her the same story. She said she'd come by at seven o'clock," Bruce said.

"How's she feeling?" asked Elizabeth in concern.

"Oh, she's fine. A little under the weather," he added for Jessica's benefit.

Jessica pretended not to hear.

"Hey, you guys," said Roger, coming into the living room.

"Hey, Rog," said Elizabeth, taking in his running gear. "Just been for a run?" Roger's cheeks were flushed, and his body was covered in perspiration.

"Yeah," he said, "five miles. It's brutal in this heat."

175

"Hey, cuz, you mind running on out of here?" Bruce asked rudely. "We've got some work to do."

"Oh, sure," said Roger. "See you, guys." He waved and jogged out of the room.

"OK," said Elizabeth, glancing around the house. "Bruce, why don't you and I hit the attic? And Jessica, you take the living room."

Jessica nodded and began looking around the living room with purpose. Bruce and Elizabeth climbed the three flights of stairs to the attic. Once there, Bruce clicked on the light and they began to sort through boxes and trunks.

Elizabeth cast a sidelong glance at Bruce, wondering if he felt as uncomfortable as she did. She thought back to the week before, when they had been together in the Patmans' attic looking for clues about their parents' college romance. The air had been practically crackling with electricity, with unspoken thoughts hanging heavily like unfulfilled promises. *And now, nothing,* thought Elizabeth with relief. Bruce was just the same old stuffy Bruce, and she was the same old straight and narrow Elizabeth. Weren't they?

Elizabeth shook the thoughts away and turned back to the cardboard box she was going through. At the bottom of the carton was a blue flowered cloth box. Elizabeth pulled it out and lifted the lid, stirring up a cloud of dust. Waving the dust away, she lifted some white tissue paper and drew out a bundle of letters wrapped in a light-pink satin ribbon.

Elizabeth untied the delicate satin ribbon and looked through the faded sheets of paper, now brittle and yellow with age. "Old love letters," she exclaimed, drawing in her breath. "From your dad to your mom.

"'Marie, how I miss you,'" she read from one. "'Only five more days of summer and then I can hold you in my arms again.'"

Bruce took the letter from her. He shook his head as he glanced through the letter. "Who would have ever thought my father could be so sappy?"

"Bruce, it's not sappy," said Elizabeth. "It's *romantic*."

"Romantic!" Bruce snorted, turning back to his trunk. "Well, save it if you think we can use it. All I have here are old ski clothes," he said, rummaging through the trunk. He picked out an old college letter sweater of his father's and held it up for size. "Nah," he said, throwing the sweater back into the trunk and shutting the lid. "Junk," he muttered, quickly going through the contents of another trunk. "Nothing here, either." He let the lid fall and opened a third trunk.

"Pay dirt!" Bruce exclaimed, gazing into it. He pulled out a bundle of yellow metro tickets and stationery from the Carlyle Hotel.

Elizabeth kneeled by him and drew in her breath. "It's stuff from their honeymoon in Paris!" she said, pulling out a paper scroll and carefully unrolling it. "A portrait of your mother!" she said, holding it up for Bruce to see. "See how young she looks with her hair long!"

Bruce pulled out a handful of ticket stubs. "L'Opéra," he said, reading the names written on the tickets, "La Comédie Française, Le Ballet de l'Opéra de Paris . . ."

177

"Wow," said Elizabeth. "They really went in style." She pulled out a large blue cotton blanket. Some white candles tumbled to the ground. "Why do you think this is in here?" she asked.

"Maybe for stuffing," guessed Bruce.

"Yeah, but the candles?" Elizabeth asked, setting the blanket aside. She reached to the bottom of the trunk and took out a handful of brochures. "The Louvre, Nôtre Dame, the Arc de Triomphe, the Eiffel Tower . . . looks like they were busy," said Elizabeth, flipping through the booklets.

"Hey, pictures!" Bruce exclaimed upon discovering a pile of black-and-white snapshots in a cardboard box.

Elizabeth looked over Bruce's shoulder as he flipped through the pictures. "It's so romantic," she breathed. "Paris! They look so young and in love. . . ."

"Look what I found!" Jessica called, rushing up the attic steps. Breathless, she crashed into the room.

"What?" Elizabeth asked.

"Geez, it's huge up here," said Jessica, looking around the enormous attic. She held up an armful of old phonograph albums.

"Hey, where'd you find those?" asked Bruce. "That's my parents' old record collection."

"In the breakfront in the living room. And look!" Jessica said, proudly displaying some ancient Beatles albums.

"Would you look at that," Elizabeth said, reading through the titles. "I know all these—*Rubber Soul, Sergeant Pepper's Lonely Hearts Club Band, Revolver, Help!* . . ."

"Let me see those," said Bruce. He ran a finger down the titles on the back. "'All You Need Is

Love.' That's it. That's their favorite song."

"Now what?" said Jessica.

"Now we haul all this stuff to the screening room, that's what," Elizabeth answered.

Jessica groaned and plopped down onto the clutter on the floor. "I was afraid you were going to say that," she said.

"Wow, look at this place," Jessica said in awe, taking in the sleek ultramodern room complete with a movie projector and screen. "I haven't been in here in ages. Did you guys redecorate?"

"Yeah. My mom decided to go for the futuristic look," said Bruce.

Elizabeth surveyed the stack of goods piled on the floor. "Let's see," she said, sifting through the material. "We've got love letters, honeymoon souvenirs, pictures, old records, home movies. . . ."

"It's all so magical." Jessica sighed, fingering the old love letters.

"Don't get all weepy on us, Wakefield," Bruce warned, then sneezed. "Ugh, we need to dust this stuff off."

"Okay. We'll do that in a minute. Now, does everybody have their roles straight?" asked Elizabeth, pacing back and forth and rubbing her hands together.

"You and I are the narrators, and Bruce is the slick behind-the-scenes director," Jessica droned. They had been over all this a million times.

"Right," said Elizabeth. She glanced at her watch nervously. "It's already ten o'clock. Do you think we should go?"

"We've probably got almost another hour," said Bruce.

"OK, let's do a quick run-through," suggested Elizabeth. "The Patmans arrive tomorrow night at seven, and Bruce brings them into the screening room."

"And 'All You Need Is Love' is playing on the stereo," said Jessica. "The memorabilia and souvenirs from their honeymoon are displayed on the coffee table."

"Right. Then we say something like, 'Welcome to your wedding,' or 'We're taking you on a trip down memory lane,'" said Elizabeth.

"Then Bruce projects the pictures of their wedding and honeymoon on the screen," Jessica said.

"Right. And while Bruce projects, we provide the narration," said Elizabeth. "We say something like, 'It's a beautiful July day, and Hank and Marie are at the altar.' And 'Hank and Marie at the reception,' 'Hank and Marie in Paris.'"

"I don't know," Bruce said, shaking his head. "Don't you think this is too much?"

"Bruce, it's our only option at this point," Jessica reminded him.

"I hope you two know what you're doing," he said skeptically.

"Then we end with home movies, the ones of when you were a baby," said Elizabeth to Bruce.

"Yeah—back when you were still cute, before they regretted having you," Jessica said sardonically. She pretended to cower as Bruce started to hover over her menacingly.

"Yeah, but I can't find our old movie projector

anywhere. Maybe Dad got rid of it," Bruce said. "I thought he had transferred all these movies to video, but if he did, I can't find them, either. I know," he said suddenly. "I'll rent a movie projector tomorrow. From the video place in Bridgewater."

"Great idea," said Elizabeth. "So we show the home movies, and then Hank grabs Marie in her arms and says, 'I love you, Marie.'"

"And Marie says, 'Oh, Hank, I love you, too,'" said Jessica.

"And everything ends happily ever after," finished Elizabeth.

"I hope you're right," Bruce grumbled, his head in his hands.

Chapter 15

Jessica lay in the bathtub Monday after dinner, luxuriating in a foam bath. She was trying to relax before the evening extravaganza.

This is really our final chance, Jessica thought. She felt anxious about the night to come. Elizabeth was fed up with her, particularly after the tape incident, and Bruce had lost all faith in her. This was her last opportunity to prove to them that she really could get Bruce's parents back together. *Well,* she thought with determination, *there's no way tonight's plan can fail.* She would show them that she was still the queen of scheming.

Jessica turned her thoughts to happier matters, envisioning her date with Michael on Tuesday. She could just imagine the night: a romantic candlelight dinner at the Beach Café, a moonlight walk on the beach afterward, their first kiss.

Jessica imagined the moment as if she were looking at a movie screen. She pictured Michael standing coolly against the crashing waves, a dark, silent James Dean with a cigarette dangling from his mouth. *No,* she thought, *scratch the cigarette. Bad breath.* Anyway, he watched as she drove up in her Jeep, her long blond hair flying. They embraced, silhouetted against the moonlight. Jessica settled dreamily in the bubbles, her feet playing lazily with the bathtub faucet.

Jessica leaned back comfortably and felt a pull at her toe. She pulled again gently, then harder. As she realized what was happening, her eyes opened in horror. Her toe was stuck in the faucet!

"Liz!" Jessica screamed. "Liz!"

"What is it?" Elizabeth said, flying into the bathroom. It was like walking into a sauna. The room was steamy from the hot water in the tub and the mirrors were fogged over. "Jessica! At a time like this, you're taking a—"

"Liz, my toe is stuck!" Jessica cried.

Elizabeth leaned down to inspect the situation.

"You're letting cold air in!" Jessica complained, shivering in the tub.

Elizabeth slammed the bathroom door shut and examined Jessica's toe. It was stuck, all right. She took Jessica's foot in her hand and tugged gently, but couldn't ease it out.

"It hurts," Jessica wailed. Her toe was beginning to swell and turn purple. "Ohmigod," she said, looking down at her toe in horror. "What if it cuts off the circulation? I could get gangrene. They might have to cut it off." Her blue-green eyes welling with hysterical tears, she leaned back and tugged furiously at the faucet, slipping down in the tub and disappearing under the bubbles.

"Jessica!" Elizabeth screamed. Jessica came up spluttering and coughing, her face covered in soapy bubbles.

"OK, Jess, calm down now," Elizabeth said, kneeling by her. "I'll hold on to your shoulders, and we'll both pull. Ready? One, two, three!"

On the count of three, both girls pulled back, yanking Jessica's toe out of the faucet. Jessica flew back against the tile wall, spraying the room with bubbles and covering Elizabeth in water.

"Oh, thank heavens," Jessica moaned. "But my poor toe feels broken." She examined it closely. "You scratched it," she accused Elizabeth.

"Sorry, Ms. Ingratitude. Put a Band-Aid on it," Elizabeth said sarcastically. "You're the one who put her toe in the faucet."

Jessica primly clambered out of the tub and grabbed a white terry-cloth robe. "Well, thank you, anyway," she said coolly.

"Now, c'mon," said Elizabeth, grabbing a towel for herself. "We haven't got any time to waste." She turned the knob to her bedroom and pulled. The door didn't budge. She pulled harder. Trying to remain calm, she tried the door leading to Jessica's bedroom. It was sealed tight.

Elizabeth stared at Jessica with a look of horror on her face. The bathroom doors must have gotten steamed shut while Jessica was in her bath, Elizabeth realized. That had happened sometimes when the weather was particularly humid. And nobody was home. Mr. and Mrs. Wakefield had gone out to dinner, leaving the girls a casserole they had heated up. They wouldn't be back for at least another hour.

Elizabeth began pounding on the door in vain. "Help, somebody help! Help!"

Jessica sighed and fell back into the tub, robe and all.

Bruce stood at the side of his Porsche, kicking the fender repeatedly while waiting for the motor club to arrive. He stared at the car resentfully. How could his baby fail him at a time like this? He was on his way back from Bridgewater, where he had rented a projector from Bridgewater Camera and Classics.

Everything had been going perfectly until he realized he had a flat tire. *No problem,* he'd thought, jacking up the car on the shoulder of the road, cars whizzing by him on the crowded freeway. *I can handle this.* Then he discovered his spare had a flat too. *Just my luck,* he had thought despairingly. *I need a spare tire for my spare tire!*

Bruce leaned back against the jacked-up car and exhaled deeply, looking around for the familiar motor-club tow truck to arrive. He glanced at his watch. Six thirty. Then he looked up at the sky. A few early stars twinkled at him knowingly. *Maybe Jessica's right,* he thought. Maybe the movement of the planets really was affecting his destiny. He sighed. He'd lost his girlfriend, his mother had moved out, and now his parents were getting a divorce. *I guess it's fate,* he thought. *My life is going downhill.*

At a little before seven o'clock, Marie Patman walked into the Patman mansion and stood for a moment in the enormous high-ceilinged foyer. She looked up at the crystal chandelier glittering brilliantly above her, feeling like a stranger in the imposing mansion.

"Bruce?" she called, walking down the long hall to the kitchen. The sound of her voice reverberated in the silent house. Mrs. Patman made her way into the kitchen, wondering where Bruce and Roger were. Her husband's Burberry raincoat was flung carelessly over a kitchen chair. Mrs. Patman instinctively picked it up and headed to the hall closet to put it away. As she walked to the closet, a key ring fell out of the pocket and clanged to the floor. She leaned over to pick it up. It was a small gold key ring with a rectangular plastic disk that had "Jessica" written on it in bright pink cursive letters. Mrs. Patman reached into the pocket of the jacket to see if anything else was there and pulled out Alice Wakefield's pink chiffon scarf. She stared baffled at the two items in her hand, then checked the tag on the label. BRUCE PATMAN.

It was Bruce's coat! Mrs. Patman walked back into the kitchen and fell hard into a chair, struck with the enormity of her realization.

Just then the front door opened and she heard footsteps coming down the hall. "Bruce?" Mrs. Patman asked. Henry Patman appeared in the doorway of the kitchen. "Henry!" Marie gasped, shocked to see her husband. "What are you doing here?"

"I might ask you the same thing," Mr. Patman replied coldly.

"Uh, Bruce called me yesterday," Mrs. Patman explained, feeling like an intruder once again. "He said he wanted to meet me alone in the screening room to talk."

"Well, he told me the same thing," said Mr.

Patman in an icy tone. "So I guess he'll know where to find me." He turned and walked out of the kitchen.

Mrs. Patman sat for a few minutes, her heart pounding in her chest. How had it all come to this? she wondered. Was it too late to save their marriage? *Well,* she thought with determination, *there's only one way to find out.* She patted her shining black hair and straightened her Chanel suit. Then she stood up and took a deep breath, holding her head high and walking out of the room.

"Henry?" Mrs. Patman said hesitatingly as she walked into the screening room. Her husband was seated on the plush sofa, drumming his fingers on the arm. Mrs. Patman sat down carefully on the opposite side of the couch.

"What?" said Mr. Patman gruffly, looking straight ahead.

Mrs. Patman searched for a way to explain the situation, but she found herself at a loss for words. "Why do you think Bruce called us here tonight?" she asked instead.

"I have no idea, but this stuff sure looks suspicious," said Mr. Patman, fingering the wedding album and scrapbooks displayed on the coffee table.

"He's gathered together all our wedding memories and laid them out in front of us," said Mrs. Patman, touched at the gesture.

"Well, I think I'd rather repress those memories at the moment," said Mr. Patman brusquely. He stood up abruptly and walked across the room to the stereo on the shelf. He picked up the needle distractedly and set it on the record. Early Beatles music began coming out of the speakers.

Mrs. Patman winced at her husband's words. "Henry, about that scarf—" she began.

Mr. Patman waved her words away with a sweep of his arm. "Forget it, Marie. If you don't believe me, you don't believe me, and there's nothing I can do about it."

"But, Henry, I do believe you," Mrs. Patman cried, the words rushing out. "You see, I just found the coat with the scarf in it. It was Bruce's coat. You had taken Bruce's coat by mistake."

But Mr. Patman wasn't listening. He walked back and forth across the room, pacing in time to the music. "There's nothing more to talk about," he said, his jaw set in a hard line. "A marriage without trust is no marriage at all."

Mrs. Patman jumped up to stand next to him. "Henry, I do trust you," she said, tears streaming down her face. "I trust you and I love you. I love you with all my heart."

Suddenly Mr. Patman stopped pacing, stunned by his wife's words. "What did you just say?" he asked, turning to look at her.

"I said that I love you and—" Mrs. Patman stuttered.

"Did you say that you trust me?" Mr. Patman asked.

"I did," she said, a glimmer of hope appearing in her eyes.

"Marie," he said softly, his eyes moist, "that means more to me than anything in the world." He went up to his wife and folded her in his arms. He drew her face toward his and kissed her tenderly.

"Henry," said Mrs. Patman after they'd pulled

apart. "Do you hear what's playing on the stereo?"

Hank Patman listened for a moment, then smiled.

"It's not true that 'all you need is love,'" Marie said. "You need trust, too. Oh, Henry, I'm so sorry about all this. I never should have doubted you."

"Well, now I see that you had every reason to doubt me," said Mr. Patman reassuringly. "But never again. That's all in the past now, right?"

Mrs. Patman nodded, smiling happily.

"We'll have to move to bigger and better things. Like—a movie, perhaps?" asked Mr. Patman.

"That's a great idea," agreed Mrs. Patman.

"How about *Breakfast at Tiffany's*, Mrs. Patman?" Mr. Patman suggested. It was one of their all-time favorites. They had watched it together on their first date, at an old drive-in theater at college.

"Sounds perfect, Mr. Patman," she said, her eyes shining with happiness.

Bruce sat on the front stoop dejectedly. He had finally been towed by the motor club and deposited at his doorstep. *Where is everyone?* he thought, looking at his watch. It was almost eight thirty, and the only cars in the driveway were those of his parents.

Just then he saw Jessica and Elizabeth roaring up in their Jeep. They pulled up in the driveway and jumped out of the car, running toward him.

"Bruce!" Elizabeth exclaimed. "We're so sorry! We had an, uh," she hesitated, "an uh, emergency situation." They had finally managed to break the seal on the bathroom doors by opening the window and running cold water in the shower.

Bruce waved away her explanation. "Don't worry

about it," he said despondently. "I just got here my-self. Flat tire. So," he said, squaring his shoulders and taking a deep breath, "ready to storm the barracks?"

The three conspirators quietly opened the front door, looking for the Patmans. Bruce shrugged and led the way around the first floor, but there was no sign of them.

Finally the only room left was the screening room. The twins put their ears to the door, but it was silent inside. Then they heard muffled voices, and what sounded like arguing. Frowning, Bruce burst into the screening room, Jessica and Elizabeth close behind. He stopped suddenly, stunned at the sight that greeted him. Mr. and Mrs. Patman were locked in a passionate embrace on the love seat. On the large TV in front of them, Audrey Hepburn was screaming at some actor Bruce didn't recognize.

The Patmans looked up, startled, and separated quickly.

"Bruce! Jessica and Elizabeth!" said Mrs. Patman ,looking flustered. "What's going on?"

"I—" Jessica began.

"We—" Bruce and Elizabeth started to explain in a rush at the same time.

"You see, we just wanted—" Bruce began again, but his voice dropped off as he searched for the words.

"We just thought—" Elizabeth said, trying to pick up from Bruce.

Mrs. Patman eyed the Wakefield twins oddly. "You know," she began, turning to Mr. Patman, "it seems like a strange coincidence that our lawyers *both* had car trouble the day we were scheduled to meet them last week."

191

Bruce looked at Elizabeth and Jessica and sank down in the sofa, bracing himself for what was to come. Jessica and Elizabeth followed his lead, sitting down next to him and looking at Marie Patman nervously.

"And it seems a *little* odd that someone filled Marie's house with flowers using *my* credit card," agreed Mr. Patman, looking at Bruce. Bruce squirmed and looked away.

"You know, come to think of it," said Mrs. Patman, "I found a *very* strange anonymous tape in my mailbox this morning." Jessica's face turned bright red.

"And somebody's key chain," continued Mrs. Patman, taking Jessica's keys out of her bag and handing them to her. Jessica took the keys silently and looked down at the floor.

"And now," concluded Mr. Patman, "here we all are together! What do you think of that?" The Patmans looked at the three kids, who were huddled together on the couch.

Bruce stared back at his parents, speechless. Then he turned to Elizabeth, his eyes silently calling for help.

"Uh, we have a history project to work on!" Elizabeth said frantically, yanking Jessica and Bruce up off the couch.

"Yeah," said Bruce. "See you later!" The three of them backed out of the room, waving and smiling as Mr. and Mrs. Patman watched them with amusement.

"It worked, it worked!" said Jessica, jumping up

192

and down in excitement as soon as they were safely out of earshot in Bruce's bedroom. "I knew I could do it! I'm the queen of schemes!"

Bruce rolled his eyes, and Elizabeth fell back onto the bed, pretending to faint from exasperation.

Chapter 16

Bruce drove along Valley Crest Drive on his way to school on Wednesday in high spirits. He rolled down the suntop and leaned his head back, enjoying the feel of the fresh morning air whipping through his hair. The heat wave had finally broken, and his parents were back together. His mother had already moved back home.

Bruce whistled happily as he coasted into the parking lot at Sweet Valley High. Now that his parents were taken care of, he thought as he pulled expertly into a parking spot and cut the engine, it was time to take care of himself. He jumped out of the car and headed toward the tennis courts.

When he got there, he saw Pamela sitting on the bench. She was watching a game in action, waiting for her turn to play. "Hi, Pamela," he said softly, sitting down next to her.

Pamela turned her head in surprise. "Oh, hi, Bruce," she said flatly. She turned back to the game, watching intently as the ball was lobbed back and forth across the net.

"Pamela, do you think we could talk for a minute?" Bruce said. He looked at her intently, a searching expression in his eyes.

"Sure, talk away," said Pamela, shrugging her shoulders.

"I came here to explain why I've been spending so much time with Elizabeth," Bruce began. Pamela listened in silence as Bruce told her about the series of plans he and the Wakefield twins had come up with to get his parents back together. By the time he got to the final intervention plan, Pamela was laughing out loud.

"Not that I think it's funny that your car broke down," Pamela explained, wiping tears of laughter from her eyes. "It's just unbelievable that so many things could go wrong."

"I know," said Bruce, shaking his head. "It was one disaster after another. Jessica ought to change her name from Wakefield to Minefield."

"So what finally happened?" Pamela asked, her voice turning serious.

"Well, I think they worked things out themselves," Bruce said. "I guess my father finally came through. My mother moved back home yesterday, and they're planning a second honeymoon to Paris."

"Oh, Bruce," Pamela said, her eyes shining. "I'm so happy for you."

"Well, I'm happy too," said Bruce, "but not completely. There's just one thing missing."

"What's that?" Pamela asked, smiling up at him.

"You," Bruce said, pulling her close and kissing

her. Pamela kissed him back. "Not anymore," she said, her voice light. She smiled as his eyes lit up with happiness and relief.

"Hey, Pamela?" he asked, running a hand down her glossy black hair. "What's the score?"

"Hmm," she said, pretending to look out at the courts. "I think its love-love," she said with a smile, her big blue eyes glowing.

"It was a total disaster," Jessica said, filling Elizabeth in on the details of her date with Michael the night before. They were sitting together alone in the cafeteria eating area at lunch on Wednesday.

"What do you mean?" asked Elizabeth.

"What I mean is—*he's* a total disaster," Jessica elaborated, stealing a fry from Elizabeth's tray. She adjusted her sunglasses on her nose and crossed her legs calmly. "I've never seen such a klutz in all my life."

"Really? Michael Hampton?" Elizabeth asked, feigning surprise. "And you thought he was so cool."

"Nope," said Jessica, taking some more fries from Elizabeth's plate. "We had him all wrong. He's shy, reserved, and extremely awkward."

"Jessica!" Elizabeth exclaimed. "Do you think you're the only one around here who has to eat?"

"Sorry," Jessica said, munching on the fries. "Chicken sandwich?" she asked, offering Elizabeth a bite.

"No, thanks," said Elizabeth, waving the sandwich away. "So what did you do?"

"Lila! Over here!" Jessica screamed, waving an arm frantically. Lila looked around and spotted them. "Getting the scoop on the latest and greatest date?" Lila asked when she sat down.

"It's very exciting," Elizabeth said with a grin.

"We-ll, we went to the Dairi Burger, where Michael spilled his chocolate shake all over me—"

"Hey, Wakefield!" Bruce called to Jessica from the next table, "get stuck in any lockers lately?"

"It's better than being stuck on yourself," Jessica retorted. A few boys at Bruce's table snickered.

"Looks like Bruce is back to his old self," Elizabeth said with a smile.

"Yeah," agreed Jessica, "now that we got his parents back together."

"Well, I don't know if we can take credit for that," Elizabeth said.

Jessica shrugged her shoulders.

"I think you guys discovered the real lesson to be learned from Mercury being in retrograde," Lila announced.

"Which is?" prompted Elizabeth.

"Which is that you can't control destiny," Lila said.

"That's for sure," Elizabeth agreed, thinking of her unfortunate affair with Bruce the week before. "So, he spills a chocolate shake on you . . ." she prompted.

"Right," said Jessica. "Then he falls all over himself trying to clean it up, pouring water all over my shirt and rubbing it with napkins—"

Lila laughed. "And then?"

"Then he gets this brilliant idea to take a romantic walk on the beach, and on the way there we get into a car accident—"

"Oh, no!" Elizabeth exclaimed. "Did anyone get hurt?"

"No, just a fender-bender," said Jessica. "So we finally make it to the beach. We take our shoes off and are walking along the coast, when Michael steps on a jellyfish—a *poisonous* jellyfish. To which he's especially allergic."

"Oh, gross," said Lila, grimacing. "Squish."

"How awful!" Elizabeth exclaimed. "What did you do?"

"Well, I drive him in his car to the emergency room at the hospital, hoping that he won't die on the way. And while they're soaking his foot and injecting him with antihistamines, one of the interns says, 'Hey, does someone have a chocolate milk shake in here?'"

"Poor Michael!" Elizabeth said, laughing.

"Poor Michael! Poor *me*!" Jessica said indignantly.

"Then you went home?" asked Elizabeth.

"Then we called his parents and they came to get us at the hospital and they drove me home," said Jessica. "And you know what the worst part of it is?"

"What?" Elizabeth asked.

"His father has already cast his movie," Jessica said.

"Oh, well," said Lila diplomatically. "I guess it just wasn't meant to be."

Jessica smiled at her best friend. "I guess it wasn't in the stars," she said, her eyes twinkling.

In the next Sweet Valley High three-part miniseries, Jessica and Elizabeth go to London to find romance and end up finding terror instead. Be sure not to miss Sweet Valley High #104, **LOVE AND DEATH IN LONDON.**

Bantam Books in the Sweet Valley High series
Ask your bookseller for the books you have missed

Life after high school gets even sweeter!

Jessica and Elizabeth are now freshman at Sweet Valley University, where the motto is: Welcome to college – welcome to freedom!

Don't miss any of the books in this fabulous new series.

♡ College Girls #1 ....56308-4 $3.50/4.50 Can.
♡ Love, Lies and Jessica Wakefield #2........56306-8 $3.50/4.50 Can.